EGYPTIAN CHRONICLES

THE
SACRED
SCARAB

Hopi and Isis can remember the terrible accident on the River Nile, when they lost their parents to crocodiles. Hopi still bears crocodile teethmarks on his leg. But five years have passed, and they've been lucky: eleven-year-old Isis is a beautiful dancer, and she's been spotted by a dance and music troupe in the town of Waset. Now they live with the troupe, and Isis performs regularly. Meanwhile, thirteen-year-old Hopi, marked by the gods, pursues his strange connection with dangerous creatures . . .

Join them in the world of ancient Egypt as they uncover the dark deeds happening around them. If there's anything you don't understand, you may find an explanation at the back of the book.

EGYPTIAN CHRONICLES

THE
SACRED
SCARAB

GILL HARVEY

BLOOMSBURY

LONDON BERLIN NEW YORK

Bloomsbury Publishing, London, Berlin and New York

First published in Great Britain in February 2010 by Bloomsbury Publishing Plc
36 Soho Square, London, W1D 3QY

A CIP catalogue record of this book is available from the British Library

ISBN 978 0 7475 9565 6

FSC
Mixed Sources
Product group from well-managed
forests and other controlled sources
Cert no. SGS - COC - 2061
www.fsc.org
© 1996 Forest Stewardship Council

Typeset by Dorchester Typesetting Group Ltd
Printed in Great Britain by Clays Ltd, St Ives plc, Bungay, Suffolk

1 3 5 7 9 10 8 6 4 2

www.bloomsbury.com/childrens
www.bloomsbury.com/gillharvey

For Florence

CONTENTS

PROLOGUE

The peasant was resting in the shade of a sprawling tamarisk tree, lying on his side with his head resting on his hand. The view was nothing special: fields of closely cropped stubble. But as the peasant gazed over them, he sighed in satisfaction. A few weeks ago, these same fields had been a sea of swaying wheat, golden ripe in the Egyptian sun. The gods had blessed him this year. The annual Nile flood had reached the perfect level, leaving behind a rich layer of silt. The seeding had gone to plan. The crop had pushed itself up eagerly and had ripened earlier than expected.

With great rejoicing, the peasant and his family had brought in the harvest and threshed and winnowed the grain. They had stored it in their mud-brick storage hut and shut the door. Then they had started to celebrate.

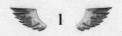 1

'Let us give thanks to the gods!' the peasant's wife had cried. 'We are going to eat well all year. We even have surplus to trade!'

The peasant had smiled to see her so happy. He smiled again now at the thought of it, and sat up. As he did so, some movement caught his eye. It was two of his sons, running full tilt in his direction.

'Father! Father!' Their voices were high with panic.

The peasant got up. 'What is it?' he called.

'They're everywhere! Thousands of them!'

'It's a plague!'

The peasant stood still. The vision of the golden wheat blowing in the breeze came into his mind, then vanished. 'A plague of what?'

'Mice, mice – they're eating their way through the store hut! Come quickly!'

The peasant picked up his stick and ran. The boys had left the store hut door open, and inside, the grain seemed alive. All over it swarmed a seething mass of rodents, squeaking and scurrying, scrambling over each other in a united feeding frenzy. The peasant gave a howl of anguish and raised his stick. Wildly, savagely he thrashed at the mice, beating and beating until his arms burned with the effort. And still they swarmed – under his feet, around his ankles, now

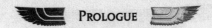

wriggling and writhing in terror.

Vaguely, the peasant was aware that the rest of his family had joined in. Neighbours, even. They used anything they could find – planks of wood, lengths of rope, smashing the furry creatures with great swinging crashes. Screams of children mingled with the squeaks and the desperate shouts of the adults . . .

At last it was over. The mice left alive fled out into the fields where they belonged. The peasant leaned against the store hut wall and stared at what was left of his harvest. How much? A quarter? A third?

He reached for the amulet that he wore around his neck. It had protected them for many years, but it had failed them now. He wrenched it loose and, in a gesture of utter despair, he hurled it to the ground.

He had not meant to break it; but, as destiny would have it, the amulet did not hit the soil, but a stone. The peasant stared down at what he had done.

'It is a sign,' he whispered.

CHAPTER ONE

Isis put her hands on her hips and stretched. Her muscles ached. In fact, she was weary all over. They'd been rehearsing day in, day out for weeks.

'Everyone ready?' asked Nefert, picking up her lute. 'Don't pull that face, Isis. You know very well how important this is.'

Isis moved into position. 'Sorry, Nefert,' she said. 'I'm just tired.'

'At your age? Nonsense.'

Nefert began plucking the lute's strings. Kia joined in on her flute, while Sheri lifted a lyre. Together the three women played a joyful melody that filled the whole house. Isis made herself concentrate again, watching Nefert carefully. When she saw a raised eyebrow, she skipped into the centre of the room and began to dance, with her partner Mut joining her

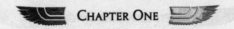

from the opposite corner. In time, the two girls swayed their hips and raised their hands high above their heads.

Somebody banged on the front door, and everyone stopped.

'*Another* interruption!' Nefert snapped. 'Who is it this time?'

'Oh, it'll be the wheat!' exclaimed Sheri. 'It's about time that arrived. Nefert, I'll have to show them the storeroom.' She put down her lyre and hurried out.

Nefert looked cross. 'Come straight back!' she called after her sister. 'We *must* get this right today. We have only five days left.'

Isis and Mut rolled their eyes at each other. As far as they were concerned, the routine was already perfect. But Nefert wouldn't let them stop practising because, for the first time ever, they were going to be part of the Beautiful Festival of the Valley that took place each year. The king himself would accompany the gods of Waset to his great mortuary temple, and Nefert was determined to make an impression.

Mut nudged Isis. 'Let's go and watch the delivery.' She turned to Nefert. 'We're just going to help Sheri, Mother.'

Nefert nodded. 'Make it quick.'

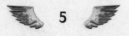

Isis grinned, and the two girls ran downstairs.

'Not there, not there!' Sheri was scolding, as a boy dumped a sack in the doorway. 'Bring it inside. Here.' She beckoned him into the storeroom.

The boy hoisted the heavy linen sack back up on to his shoulder. It was almost as big as he was, and he staggered under its weight. He shuffled in one step at a time and plonked the sack down just as a second delivery boy appeared in the doorway with another.

'This is the last one,' he said.

'Good,' said Sheri. 'Put it over here.'

Isis and Mut squeezed into the store. It smelled good in there – herbs and spices mingled with the earthy smell of grain. There were bags of barley as well as the wheat, fruits and vegetables, and a big pot of honey in one corner.

The boys left, and Mut poked at the sacks. A few grains came through the weave, and she nibbled at them.

'We'll have lovely fresh bread tomorrow, Sheri!'

'If we ever find the time to grind the grain,' said her aunt wryly. 'Come. We must get back to Nefert.'

'Do we have to? Mother's driving us too hard,' moaned Mut.

Sheri smiled gently. 'You can never practise too

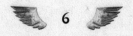

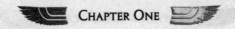

hard, Mut. You know that.' And she turned to go back to their practice room.

Mut pouted, making a larger hole in the sack with her finger.

'Come *on*!' whispered Isis, heading after Sheri. She didn't fancy making Nefert any more grumpy than she already was. But she was just climbing the stairs when she heard a loud thump on the mud-brick steps behind her. She spun around. 'Mut!'

Her dance partner was sprawled on the floor, her face twisted in pain, one hand clutching her ankle. 'Ow, ow!' she howled.

Isis rushed to Mut's side. 'What have you done? Let me see!'

Tears began to roll down Mut's cheeks. 'Those stupid delivery boys! They moved the date box and I didn't see it!'

Isis looked and saw the box just below the steps. The boys must have shifted it to make room for the sacks of grain.

Mut sat up, still crying, as Sheri reappeared on the stairs.

'Whatever's going on?' she exclaimed. 'Mut, what happened?'

'I fell,' whimpered Mut. 'I think I've broken my ankle.'

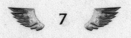

'Broken!' Sheri dropped to her knees by Mut's side. 'Don't say that. Let go, let me feel it.'

Mut squealed in pain as Sheri began to feel her way down the injured leg. Nefert and Kia appeared, and watched. No one said anything, but Isis knew only too well what everyone was thinking. This was bad news. *Very* bad news.

'Try moving it, Mut,' instructed Sheri.

'*Ah-ah!* I can't,' gasped Mut.

'Not even a little bit?'

Grimacing, Mut tried again, and Isis saw that her ankle seemed to move slightly. Sheri finished gently feeling it and looked up at the anxious faces around them.

'I don't think it's broken,' she said. 'But we should get the doctor to come and check.'

'But what about the festival routine?' asked Mut, through her tears. 'What if I can't dance?'

Nefert looked away. Isis knew there was no answer to that.

'Don't think the worst until it's happened,' said Kia briskly. 'I'll go and fetch the doctor.'

Mut's ankle had already swollen to twice its usual size. Isis felt her heart sink. The festival was such a golden opportunity. All sorts of things might come of it – it could bring the troupe work for months, even years. But if they couldn't provide dancers, their chance would be gone, and it might never again be repeated.

Very carefully, Hopi applied an ointment of mashed onion and salt to the farmer's arm. The man winced as the mash went on, then held his arm stiffly as Hopi wrapped a bandage around it.

'Will I live?' the farmer asked, his voice quaking.

Hopi grinned. 'Oh yes, you'll be fine.' He looked up at Menna. 'Won't he, Menna?'

The old priest of Serqet sighed. 'Yes, yes. This snake is harmless.'

'Harmless? But its teeth sank deep into my arm!' exclaimed the farmer.

'Trust me,' said Menna wearily, 'I see plenty of these bites at harvest time. The snake was hiding in a sheaf of wheat, am I right?'

'Yes, but . . .' The farmer looked dubious. 'You are sure, then?'

'Perfectly sure. Keep the ointment on until tomorrow, then unwrap the bandage. The bite will soon heal.'

The farmer stared at his arm, as though he could scarcely believe his luck. Then he scratched his head with his good arm, and stood up. 'I must pay you,' he said. 'I have brought grain.'

'Grain is always welcome,' said Menna. 'Though the gods know I can't seem to eat very much these days.'

The farmer indicated the bag that he had by his side. 'I hope this is enough.'

'Indeed. May the gods be with you.'

Hopi took in Menna's tired eyes and hunched shoulders as he showed the farmer out of the house. This was the busiest time of the year, but his tutor was not himself. With every new patient who arrived to receive treatment, he seemed a little more weary, a little more depressed. Hopi knew he was grieving the death of his brother, but it seemed to have affected him very deeply.

Menna returned to the courtyard. 'I'm afraid there will be no more treatments today,' he said, wiping his forehead. 'You may go, Hopi. There is something I must do.'

Hopi scrambled to his feet. 'Can't I help you, Menna?'

The old man shook his head. 'I must visit the family tomb. It is over the river on the west bank.'

This was intriguing news. 'I could carry your bag,' Hopi offered.

Menna smiled. 'I can see you won't take no for an answer. Very well, Hopi. Thank you. Fetch me my cloak – I may feel a chill on the river.'

Hopi did as his tutor told him, and they were soon making their way through the winding streets of Waset. Menna had a bad back and walked with a stoop, while Hopi had a limp from the day he had been attacked by crocodiles, so they didn't hurry. Hopi wandered along by his tutor's side, thinking. He knew that Menna's brother was lying in the embalmers' workshops, his body slowly drying out in natron salt. That should have been enough to tell him that Menna's family was rich – most people couldn't afford to give their loved ones such special treatment. But Menna had always seemed humble, and his house was not at all grand, so Hopi hadn't given it much thought. This was different – a family tomb on the west bank was impressive.

They reached the riverbank, where a ferry shunted to and fro across the Nile. Hopi helped Menna on board, and they sat waiting for the boat to fill up.

Menna seemed to be thinking, too. He turned to Hopi, placing a hand on his knee. 'I am growing old,' he said quietly. 'It is good that you have come with me.'

'You know I'd do anything to help,' said Hopi.

'Yes,' the old man sighed. 'You're a good apprentice. You have already learned much. But there are some lessons that only the gods can teach.'

Hopi looked at him. 'What sort of lessons?'

Menna shook his head. 'You will learn, Hopi, you will learn. I must ensure that you do, before it is too late. For the time being, it is good that you will see my tomb, for I, too, will lie there one day.'

The ferry started to glide across the Nile. Hopi gazed over the water at the west bank, where the barren mountains of the desert rose up against the blue sky. This was the Kingdom of the Dead, where people were taken to meet the Next World. He was burning with curiosity, and a little fear, too. He didn't like to think of Menna's death, or of anything being *too late*.

The doctor poked and pulled at Mut's leg, pushing her ankle one way and then the other, causing her to shriek with pain. Eventually, he stood up.

'I shall soothe her ankle with balm and wrap it in linen,' he announced. 'But there is nothing else to be done. The gods will heal it.' He rummaged in his bag for some bandages.

'It isn't broken?' asked Mut.

'No,' said the doctor. 'It's a sprain. You must rest it – no walking or running.'

'What about dancing?' breathed Mut.

'Absolutely no dancing.'

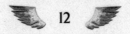

Mut started snivelling again, and Isis crouched down to put an arm around her shoulders.

Nefert's forehead was creased with anxiety. 'How soon will it heal?' she asked. 'We have only two dancers. There's no one to replace her, and the festival is in five days. Is it possible that she could take part?'

'Five days?' The doctor looked thoughtful.

Isis held her breath. She hated the thought of dancing alone.

'If she rests completely, it is possible,' said the doctor. He lifted Mut's ankle on to his knee and began wrapping the linen around it. 'But I mean *completely*. She must not walk on it at all.'

So there was hope. 'You'll get better, Mut,' whispered Isis. 'I'm sure you will. And we already know the routine.'

Mut bit her lip, trying to sniff back her tears. She nodded. 'I hope so.'

The doctor finished his bandaging, and Nefert went with him to the door.

'Thank you, doctor,' Isis heard her say. 'It's most important that she recovers quickly.'

Sheri and Isis helped Mut up on to her good leg. With their support, she managed to hop out into the courtyard to sit with Ramose and Kha, her two younger brothers.

'You can watch us all while we do the rest of the preparations,' said Sheri. 'You'll be better in no time.'

Mut just about managed to smile.

By the time Menna had crossed the fields and passed the royal mortuary temples, he seemed exhausted. Hopi was growing more and more worried about him, and feared that he wouldn't make it back to Waset.

'You have to rest,' he said to his tutor. 'Tell me where your tomb is, and what needs to be done.' He guided Menna to a boulder and made him sit down.

'Don't worry, I'll be fine.' The old man pointed in the direction of the limestone cliffs. 'Our tomb is small, nestled among the cliffs there. I must check that the seals have not been tampered with, and say some prayers in the chapel. Just give me a moment.'

Hopi waited, feeling disappointed. So he wouldn't see inside the tomb at all. He had been very near here before, with his younger sister Isis, when the troupe had visited the village of the tomb-builders. Then they had seen inside a plundered royal tomb, but the idea of seeing this one was different. It was still in use, waiting to receive new occupants; one day, Menna himself would lie there.

At last, Menna rose to his feet and began to plod

steadily towards the cemetery. He made his way surely among the chapels – some grand, some modest – until he reached one of the smallest, tucked close to the face of the rocks. They entered. It was peaceful, painted with beautiful scenes of the afterlife, and Menna looked visibly relieved to see the tomb's sealed door.

'It is safe,' he muttered, and heaved a big sigh. 'So this is not the problem.'

Hopi frowned. 'There's a problem? What do you mean?'

Menna put a hand on his shoulder. 'My brother is lying in natron. He will soon be wrapped and placed here. But something is not right. Not right.' He shook his head. 'There will be trouble before his burial is through.'

'How do you know?' Hopi was baffled. He stared around the little chapel. He couldn't see anything wrong.

But the old man was praying, his eyes closed, muttering ancient supplications under his breath. Hopi waited until he finished. When he opened his eyes again, Menna bowed his head.

'When I delivered his body to the embalmers' workshops, I sensed it,' he said, and turned towards the doorway.

Hopi walked silently by Menna's side as they made their way back to the ferry. He knew better than to ask questions; Menna would never explain anything until he was ready. And when they eventually reached Waset once more, the sun was dipping in the west, throwing long shadows along the streets. It was time to go home.

To Hopi's surprise, the house was quiet. He paused in the hallway, listening. He could hear the murmur of adult voices on the first floor: the sisters – Nefert, Sheri, Kia . . . and Paneb, Nefert's husband. Isis and Mut were usually bouncing around, but there was no sign of them. Hopi walked through to the courtyard. The two girls sat there, looking subdued, with Mut's brothers. Isis was stirring a big pot of freshly brewed beer.

'What happened?' demanded Hopi, spotting Mut's leg.

'I tripped,' said Mut miserably. 'The stupid grain delivery boys left a box jutting out in the storeroom.'

'Did the doctor do that?' asked Hopi, nodding at the bandages.

'Yes. He says I have to rest it completely.'

Hopi looked at Isis. He had a good idea how upset she must be. She'd put so much into this festival –

every night she was exhausted from practising. And it would be bad news for the whole family if they couldn't perform.

'I'll ask Menna if there's an ointment we can put on it,' he offered.

Mut pulled a face. 'Yuck!' she exclaimed. 'I don't want a snake-bite potion, Hopi! The doctor said we just have to wait.'

'I was only trying to help,' muttered Hopi. His stomach rumbled. 'Is there anything to eat? Some bread or something?'

Isis shook her head. 'All the bread's gone into the beer. Have a look in the storeroom.'

Hopi nodded glumly. He hadn't expected anything better. With all the preparations for the festival, meal-times had become very erratic. He entered the house again and peered into the storeroom. Bags of grain weren't any use when you were hungry. He opened the box of dates and stuffed one into his mouth. Then he reached for a ripe fig from the fruit store. But, as he did so, he heard a noise. He stood still for a moment, listening. There it was again – someone was knocking on the door. It was an odd time for visitors. Frowning, Hopi went to see who it was.

A gaunt-looking man stood on the street outside. Hopi stared at him. He was dressed in the coarse linen worn mostly by peasants, and his hands were rough and grimy.

'Greetings,' said the man, his voice low and shaky. 'May the gods be with you. Is this the house of Paneb, son of Amenakht?'

'Well . . . yes,' said Hopi. He couldn't imagine what a peasant wanted with Paneb.

The man shifted from one foot to the other. He cast his eyes to the ground, then looked up at Hopi again. 'He *is* here?'

'Yes, he's here,' said Hopi. The man was making him uncomfortable. 'Who should I say you are? I'll go and get –'

'No!' the peasant almost shouted. 'Wait . . . wait a moment.' He looked at the ground again, as though composing his thoughts. Then he looked up again with something like determination in his eyes. 'Please let me come in. I do not wish to greet my cousin on the street.'

'Cousin!'

'You may tell Paneb that his cousin Sinuhe needs to speak with him.'

'Of . . . of course,' said Hopi hurriedly, taken aback. He opened the door wider. 'Come and sit in the front room. I'll fetch him for you.'

Sinuhe stepped inside, his eyes wide and curious,

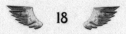

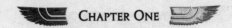

as though he had never been to the house before. Hopi led him into the room that the family reserved for guests.

'Wait here,' he said, and made his way upstairs to the room where the adults were talking.

'There's a man here,' he announced. He looked at Paneb. 'He says he's a relative – your cousin Sinuhe.'

Silence fell. The women looked at each other, then at Paneb, their expression stunned. But, if anything, Paneb looked even more surprised.

'Who is this man?' Nefert demanded.

'I . . . I can explain,' said Paneb. But, as he got to his feet, Hopi saw that his eyes said something else. Perhaps he *could* explain, but he certainly didn't want to.

CHAPTER TWO

Isis heard Hopi talking.

'We've got a visitor,' she said, scrambling to her feet. She handed the stirring spoon to Ramose. 'I'll go and see who it is.'

Hopi had already disappeared up the stairs. Tiptoeing forward, Isis peeked into the guest room and saw a man sitting with his head bowed. His skin was a deep, deep brown from long hours working in the sun, and his kilt was shabbier than anything Paneb or Hopi would wear. His toenails were deeply ingrained, not with the dust of Waset, but with the rich black earth of the surrounding farmland.

Paneb came jumping down the stairs two at a time, and Isis shrank back, out of the way. Nefert, Kia and Sheri followed more slowly, with Hopi limping behind them. Isis met her brother's gaze and, together, they sidled up to the doorway to watch.

Sinuhe stood up as Paneb entered. 'Cousin Paneb,' he murmured, 'may the gods be with you. It is too long since we last met.'

'Cousin Sinuhe,' Paneb responded. 'It has indeed been a long time. What brings you into Waset? Are you and your family well?'

'We are quite well, thank you,' said Sinuhe. 'For that, at least, we can be grateful.' He hesitated. He looked at the three beautiful women standing behind Paneb, then around the front room with its murals, wooden chairs and caskets. 'I see that you, too, are well, cousin. The gods have blessed you.'

Paneb's face hardened. 'Yes. We are fortunate, cousin Sinuhe,' he said. 'But make no mistake: it is the result of hard work.'

'No doubt,' Sinuhe responded. 'I did not come to suggest –'

'Good. Pray, tell us why you have come,' Paneb interrupted him. 'Only something of the greatest importance can have brought you here.' He gestured at the chairs. 'Please sit.'

The peasant lowered himself back down. 'The gods have given me a sign. You must understand – it is they who have sent me, cousin Paneb.'

Paneb looked at him shrewdly. 'You've come begging, haven't you?'

'No!' The word burst from the peasant's lips. Then his confidence seemed to waver. His gaze slid away, down to the ground. 'Well, we are desperate, cousin, but I would not have come if the gods had not willed it.'

Isis stared at him, fascinated. He seemed humble but proud, respectful but angry, all at the same time.

'Go on,' said Paneb, his voice relenting a little. 'Explain yourself. What has befallen you?'

Sinuhe straightened his back again. 'As you know, our farmland is south of Waset,' he said. 'We grow emmer wheat. Each year, the tax collectors come and measure the fields to decide how big our harvest will be. Then they tell us how much we must pay in tax.'

Isis had heard that the king's stores were piled high with the best grain in the country, but she'd never quite realised how it got there.

'The tax collectors often demand more than they should,' said Sinuhe. 'We are used to that. We are used to them shifting the boundaries, then moving them back again when it suits them. But this year . . .' he trailed off.

'What has happened?' Paneb asked quietly.

Sinuhe clasped and unclasped his hands, and took

a few shallow, gulping breaths. 'A plague,' he whispered. 'A plague of mice.'

The room went still.

'We thought we were lucky,' Sinuhe carried on. 'We had a bumper crop – we even harvested early, earlier than all our neighbours. The stores of grain were waiting for Abana and his men, and then –'

'Abana?' Paneb interrupted. 'I know that name.'

'He is the new chief tax collector. They say he has come from the north.'

Paneb seemed to stiffen, but he said nothing.

'Tell us about the mice,' prompted Sheri.

Sinuhe's hands began to tremble. 'During the time that our grain was stored, they multiplied,' he said. 'But we didn't even notice them until it was too late. They were hidden in the depths of the store, breeding and feeding . . . feasting.'

'How much of the crop was lost?'

'We managed to salvage some of it.' He shook his head. 'But, in fact, this was our greatest misfortune.'

Paneb looked puzzled. 'How?'

'We hoped that the tax collectors would be reasonable. But when they saw that we had some grain, they demanded the full amount of tax. We protested, but there was nothing we could do. They took everything – our whole crop.'

Silence fell. Paneb stroked his chin. Isis could tell that the story disturbed him deeply but, at the same time, she saw doubt on his face.

'And what is it that you want me to do, cousin?' he asked eventually.

'Cousin Paneb, you are a man of Waset,' said Sinuhe. 'You are wealthy, with many connections. Give me some of your grain to tide us over. And, I beg you, use your influence to bring us justice.'

Paneb looked genuinely astonished. '*Wealthy?*' he echoed. 'This is madness. We are not rich! We are performers – we never know from one week to the next where our food is coming from.'

Isis saw disbelief spread across Sinuhe's face. 'But . . .' He gestured around him. 'Cousin, you say this, and yet you live in ease and comfort.'

Paneb's face darkened. 'You think our life is easy?'

'Try toiling under the sun, cousin.' Sinuhe's voice had a bitter edge to it. 'That is what you –'

'Enough!' Paneb's voice boomed, and the peasant seemed to cower before him.

Isis saw Nefert shoot a glance at her husband. She stood up and smoothed her hands over her white gown. 'I see you are troubled and tired,' she said to the stranger. 'No doubt you are hungry, too. Let us give you something to eat and drink. When you have rested, we can speak of this again.' She turned around. 'Isis, go and fetch some beer. Hopi, take some grain from the store and buy fresh bread from a neighbour.'

Paneb gave a little nod of agreement to his wife and the taut features of the peasant softened a little.

'Thank you,' he said. He licked his dry, cracked lips. 'I am very grateful.'

Hopi and Isis hurried out of the room, and dived inside the storeroom so that they could speak.

'What a story!' gasped Isis. 'Do you believe him?'

Hopi looked at her in surprise. It had never crossed his mind that Sinuhe might be lying. After their parents had died, he and Isis had known all about poverty and hunger. Perhaps his sister was too young to remember, but he could recognise the symptoms only too well.

'Yes,' he whispered. 'He's telling the truth, Isis. Why wouldn't he be?'

Isis pursed her lips. 'Didn't you see? Paneb doesn't like him at all.'

'Perhaps. But that doesn't mean he's lying. I believe what he said about the mice and the tax collectors.'

'Oh, I believe the mice part,' said Isis. 'But there's something funny about him, Hopi. Why hasn't he seen Paneb for all this time?'

Hopi reached for a little linen bag and scooped some grain from the top of one of the sacks. 'I don't know,' he said. 'There's bound to be a good reason.' He tied a knot in the top of the bag, and poked his sister good-humouredly. 'You'd better go and get that beer.'

'Oh yes,' she said. 'And I must tell Mut what's happened. She'll be *dying* to know.'

Hopi slipped outside on to the street, clutching the bag of grain. It was dark now. Who would have fresh bread for sale at this hour? There wasn't much call for it in this area anyway – most households made their own. He thought for a moment, then turned right towards the river and knocked on a door near the end of the street. It belonged to their neighbour Meryt-Amun, a local trader who bought and sold cedar wood from Lebanon. His work took him away from home a great deal, and his wife and daughters worked hard in his absence; weaving linen, ironing gowns into beautiful pleats, making exquisite clay-bead collars, and – sometimes – baking bread. They owed Hopi a favour, because his skill with snakes was well known locally and he had recently removed a cobra from their courtyard. It was definitely worth giving them a try.

The eldest daughter Yuya came to the door – a bubbly, lively girl a few years older than Hopi himself.

'Hopi!' she said, smiling. 'Come in.'

'I can't stay,' Hopi told her. 'I'm in a hurry. Do you have any bread for sale?'

'Bread!' Yuya looked askance. 'It's an odd time to be buying bread.'

'I know,' said Hopi. 'We have an unexpected visitor.'

At the word *unexpected*, Yuya's eyes lit up. 'Ooooh, is it someone we know?' She grinned. 'Come in. I'm in the middle of pleating something, but I'll see what we've got.'

Reluctantly, Hopi followed her inside. He knew he should be getting right back, and once the women began questioning, it would be difficult to get away. They loved nothing better than gossip.

In the courtyard, Meryt-Amun's wife was busy pounding pomegranates by the light of a couple of oil lamps.

'Hopi! It's been too long since you dropped in. Come and have some of this juice, it's fresh.'

'Thank you, but I've only come –' he began weakly.

'They have a visitor,' announced Yuya. 'He's come to buy bread.'

One of Yuya's sisters appeared, trailing a length of linen, and Hopi found himself surrounded by women.

'You're buying bread?' Meryt-Amun's wife laughed. 'At this hour? Can't your guest wait for the evening meal?'

'He's too hungry, I think,' Hopi said, then instantly regretted it. The women pounced on his words.

'Too *hungry*! Whoever is it?' quizzed Yuya.

'A relative . . . a cousin . . . I've never seen him before.' Hopi tried to keep it vague, but there was no stopping the women now.

'Whose relative? Paneb's? Where has he come from? What does he want?'

The questions came thick and fast, the women all speaking at once, and before he knew it, Hopi had spilled the whole story.

'How terrible,' said the younger daughter. 'Mice.' She shuddered.

But Meryt-Amun's wife had a curious gleam in her eyes. 'I always wondered where Paneb came from,' she said. 'We know all about Nefert, of course. Her family has lived around here for generations. But Paneb . . . hmm. Very interesting, Hopi. Now, let's see about that bread.'

With two flat loaves tucked under his arm, Hopi hurried home again, chiding himself for letting so much slip. But it had made him think, too. Perhaps Isis was right. Everyone seemed to find Sinuhe's appearance intriguing . . . maybe there was more to it, after all.

'I want to speak to everyone.' Paneb's voice was low. 'We shall all go up on to the roof, so we can be sure that Sinuhe doesn't hear.'

'He's sound asleep,' Sheri assured him. 'I laid a sheet over him. He didn't stir.'

'Even so,' said Paneb. 'This is a serious matter.' He looked around the courtyard. 'Follow me when the chores are done.'

The family was sitting outside in the moonlight, finishing the last of their meal. Ramose and Kha were sleepy, cuddled up to Nefert and Sheri. Isis mopped up the last scraping of lentil stew with some bread and popped it into her mouth. She thought of how Sinuhe had gobbled the bread they'd given him, eating it so fast he'd almost choked.

Paneb lifted Mut into his arms and carried her up the stairs while Isis helped Kia clear the pots and dishes away. Then she headed up to the roof, where Paneb was already sitting, cross-legged, with Mut propped up beside him. The family gathered around.

'What a day,' sighed Nefert. 'First Mut's ankle, and

then this . . . cousin.' She hesitated over the word *cousin*, glancing at Sheri and Kia.

Sheri addressed her brother-in-law with gentle curiosity. 'Paneb,' she said, 'you are not a peasant. You have been a man of the town for as long as we have all known you. You have never even visited the fields. How can this man claim to be kin?'

Paneb looked flustered. 'Everyone has relatives, Sheri.'

'Why, yes, but –'

'A family tree can sprout in many directions.' There was a hint of anger in Paneb's voice now.

Kia frowned. 'But that's not common. And the thought of a mere *peasant* –' She broke off, clearly appalled.

'He's a relative, and that's that,' said Paneb coldly. 'I'm sorry the thought is so distasteful to you.'

'We weren't saying that,' said Sheri gently. 'It's just . . . surprising, that's all. And of course we must help him. I'm sure we can spare a sack of grain.'

'One sack of grain will hardly solve his problems.' Paneb gazed out towards the river, then turned back to his family and took a deep breath. 'There's something else that I must tell you. We've received another request to perform – at a harvest celebration party tomorrow night.'

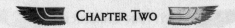

Isis felt a pang of alarm. She exchanged a worried look with Mut.

'Tomorrow! But Mut is injured –' began Nefert.

'The request is from Abana, the head of the tax collectors.'

Everyone was shocked into silence for a second.

Then Kia spoke. 'Surely that's out of the question.'

'Is it?' Paneb looked around. 'Why?'

'Paneb, don't be absurd,' said Nefert. 'For one thing, Mut can't dance for several days. The doctor has totally forbidden it. And for another, whoever Sinuhe may be, he has recently suffered at the hands of this man. How could you think of entering the house of one who has inflicted such pain?'

Isis let out a sigh of relief. She didn't mind being watched when Mut was close to her, but the thought of dancing alone was awful.

Paneb's face was grave. 'I understand the difficulties,' he said. 'I've been thinking about nothing else all evening. But we can still offer music, and Isis can perform the girls' old routine. Besides, this may be our opportunity to make contact with Abana. Perhaps we can make him see reason. Perhaps . . . perhaps the gods have willed it this way.'

This was dreadful. Isis looked beseechingly at Nefert. 'But I can't dance on my own!' she burst out.

'He will pay us handsomely,' Paneb carried on, almost as though he hadn't heard her. 'It will surely be worth our while.'

'But we all know that this tax collector is a cheat and a swindler.' Sheri's voice was hot with indignation.

'We've worked for such people before.'

'Not when we *know* those who've suffered –'

'Enough, Sheri. This may help Sinuhe, too.'

Isis couldn't bear it. 'But I *can't*!' she wailed.

'I'm afraid, Isis, that you have little choice.'

When Paneb spoke in that tone of voice, Isis knew that his mind was made up. He had brought them up to the roof to tell them, not to consult them. How could he do this to her? And why was he bending over backwards for this so-called cousin when he'd just appeared out of the blue?

CHAPTER THREE

Hopi left the house early the next morning. He wanted to tell Menna about Sinuhe and the mice, because his tutor was fascinated by all living creatures. Menna made his living from treating snake bites and scorpion stings, but his knowledge stretched much further. Hopi was sure that he would have plenty to say about a plague of mice. He might even be able to interpret it as a sign from the gods.

He found the old man sitting in his courtyard, staring at a little casket that lay at his feet. He barely looked up as Hopi approached.

'Hopi,' he murmured, 'may the gods be with you.'

'And also with you, Menna,' said Hopi, sitting down beside his master. 'I hope you are well.'

'Well enough, well enough,' said the old man,

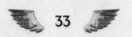

33

but his voice was weary.

Hopi hesitated. He wanted to blurt out his story, but something stopped him. 'Is there anything I can do for you, Menna? Have you eaten today?'

'Food . . .' Menna shook his head, as though the mere thought of it was off-putting.

It frightened Hopi a little. 'Master, I know you are grieving,' he said. 'But the body cannot survive on sorrow alone. You will grow weak. Let me prepare a meal for you.'

Menna lifted his head and studied Hopi with calm, soft eyes. He reached out with his thin hand and touched Hopi's arm. 'These times will pass,' he said. 'I understand your concern better than you think. I want you to do something for me.'

'Anything.' Hopi was relieved to hear more strength in the old priest's voice.

Menna reached for the casket and lifted the lid. He fished around inside and brought out a small object. 'Open your hand.'

Hopi did as he said. Menna dropped the object into his palm and Hopi looked down. All that sat there was a simple scarab amulet made out of blue faience, like the ones worn by thousands of Egyptians every day.

'What is it?' asked Menna.

Hopi frowned. 'It's just a scarab,' he said.

'A sacred scarab,' agreed Menna.

'What should I do with it?'

Menna smiled. 'You can give it back, for now.' He held out his hand and Hopi returned the amulet. 'This is only a model of the real thing. It's the real thing that I want you to seek. Go into the fields, and observe the life of the scarab.'

'Observe the . . .' Hopi stared. 'What, you mean, now?'

The old man nodded. 'Why not? The morning is a good time to walk out to the fields. And don't fret about me – I need very little to eat. I will take care of that later.'

Bewildered, Hopi got to his feet. 'But what if someone comes for treatment?'

'I've managed to treat patients on my own for many years, Hopi.' Menna looked at him wryly.

Hopi flushed. Menna could make him feel very foolish sometimes, although he knew he didn't mean to. 'Very well. I will go straight away. What do I do when I've finished?'

'Come and tell me what you've seen,' said Menna.

Hopi left the priest sitting there, and let himself out on to the street. It was only when he had set off along the winding streets leading south that he remembered – he hadn't told Menna about Sinuhe, or his tale of the plague of mice.

Ramose and Kha ran into the courtyard and rushed up to Isis and Mut.

'We saw him eat his breakfast!' squealed Kha. 'He ate it fast. Like this.' He opened his mouth wide and pretended to stuff food into it.

Isis tried to keep a straight face. But then she caught Mut's eye and they both snorted with laughter.

'He's dirty,' said Ramose. 'I don't think he knows how to wash.'

'Yes,' said Kha, his eyes wide with glee. 'He *smells*!'

Isis sucked in her cheeks, trying to make her face serious. She and Mut shouldn't encourage the boys to make fun of Sinuhe. But she couldn't blame them, either. Sinuhe was very different from any visitor they'd ever seen, and what they said was true. He *did* smell.

'You two should try to fix the toy that Kia gave you,' she said, pointing to a little wooden dog in the corner of the courtyard. Its legs were supposed to move, but they'd been stuck ever since the boys had used it in a tug of war. 'Does she know it's broken?'

Guilt spread over the boys' faces, and they rushed

to pick up the toy. Isis bent over her work again, half-heartedly grinding a batch of grain. Mut watched her for a moment, looking bored, then struggled to her feet and hopped to the courtyard door.

'Careful, Mut!' exclaimed Isis. 'Don't you dare hurt your ankle again. You've got to get better quickly.'

Mut wasn't listening to her. She was craning her neck, trying to hear what was going on inside. 'I haven't even *seen* him,' she complained. 'All this fuss about someone I haven't even met!'

'He's just a peasant,' said Isis. 'I've got to dance alone, thanks to him.'

Mut hopped back across the courtyard and flopped down. 'I bet Father would have made you dance any-way, even if he hadn't shown up.'

Isis shook her head, pushing the grain back and forth on the grinding stone. 'I'm not so sure. We have enough work at the moment.' Then she looked at her dance partner curiously. 'Do *you* know where your father came from?'

'What d'you mean?' Mut's face was sharp.

Isis hesitated. She had always taken Mut's family for granted. She and Hopi were the ones with all the problems: their parents had died a horrible death, pulled underwater by crocodiles, and then they had begged on the streets until Paneb had taken them in.

It had never occurred to her that Mut's family might have its own stories to tell.

'Well, Nefert and Sheri and Kia . . . they grew up as dancers, didn't they?' she said slowly. 'Their mother taught them to play music.'

'Yes. My grandmother taught them everything,' said Mut proudly. 'It runs in the family.'

'But not in your father's family,' suggested Isis. 'Paneb doesn't play music, does he? Well, he only keeps time, with the clappers.'

Mut clearly didn't like this line of thinking. 'So what?' she snapped. 'You don't have a father at all.'

'I know that. I wasn't saying –'

'What *are* you saying?'

Isis knew better than to push it. 'Nothing,' she sighed, and scooped up a handful of flour from the grinder. 'Come and look at this flour. Do you think it's fine enough yet?'

Hopi limped through the outskirts of Waset to the south, passing donkeys carrying vast bales of straw and others heavily loaded with grain. The harvest was almost at an end. Hopi listened to the *thwack* of boys' sticks on the donkeys' backs and gazed out over the fields, which were mostly just stubble now. It was easy to see the rich, black earth, made up of the silt that the River Nile left behind each year.

Hopi wandered on to a bare field and made his way along the edge with his eyes trained on the ground. Then he spotted what he was looking for and stopped. It was a little mound of donkey dung. He poked at it with his stick. Nothing. It was fresh; perhaps the scarabs hadn't found it yet.

He kept walking. A little further on there was another pile of dung – and, this time, it looked almost alive. Crawling all over it were about fifteen scarabs, their shiny black wings glinting in the sun. Hopi squatted down on his haunches and watched.

The beetles were working furiously. They were using the donkey dung to create perfectly round balls, each one several times the size of the beetles themselves. Hopi realised he'd never watched them closely before. It was incredible. How did they manage to make their dung balls so round? And so big? Some of them had finished making the balls and were beginning to push them away. That was amazing, too. They more or less stood on their heads and rolled their dung balls along with their hind legs. It made Hopi smile.

The pile of donkey dung was soon demolished. Some of the beetles fought, trying to claim another's hard work. But most of them kept on pushing their balls away, away, up and over ruts of earth and between stalks of corn. Hopi wondered how they knew where they were going. He followed a couple of them and found that they had burrows. Somehow, they shoved their precious balls inside, down into the earth, and covered them up.

'Hey!'

The voice made Hopi jump. He looked around. A peasant farmer was marching over the field, waving his stick.

'What are you doing here?' the man demanded. 'You're trespassing.'

'Oh, I'm sorry.' Hopi pointed at the ground. 'I was just watching some scarabs.'

'Very likely. Where are you from?'

'Just from Waset. My tutor sent me to study here – I'm training to be a priest,' Hopi told him hurriedly. 'A priest of Serqet.'

The farmer rubbed his chin. He looked doubtful, but didn't dare question Hopi's words. 'A priest, eh? Can't see why a priest needs to poke around in the bare earth.'

Hopi tended to agree with him, but he had no other explanation for being there. It would be safer to change the subject. 'Did you have a good harvest?' he asked. 'Looks like you managed to bring it all in.'

The farmer grunted and folded his arms. 'Harvest was fair enough. Rotten, cheating tax collectors, that's our problem.'

Hopi's ears pricked up. 'Really? What happened?'

'You see those markers there.' The farmer pointed to some little white stones that stretched across the field. 'Well, beyond those stones it's my neighbour's land. We've kept track of that boundary as far back as I can remember, never had a problem. Now, when that new tax collector Abana came along last week, he said they'd been moved. "According to our records." That's what he said. Showed us this big papyrus scroll all covered in marks.'

Abana. That name was cropping up a lot lately.

'And were the records correct?' asked Hopi.

The farmer shrugged. 'How should I know? The likes of us can't read.'

Of course. It was all too easy to fool someone uneducated. 'But didn't you protest?' asked Hopi.

'Didn't have a chance,' growled the farmer. 'He and his men loaded up the extra taxes and moved on. When I spoke to my neighbour, it turned out they'd played exactly the same trick on him. Dirty scoundrels.'

Hopi felt himself growing hot with indignation. Abana was the man who had cheated Sinuhe, too.

'But that's so wrong!' he exclaimed. 'These men are servants of the gods and king. They should be brought to account!'

The farmer threw him a cynical look. 'Yes, well, you're young, lad. You would say that.'

'Take this bowl of food to our cousin Sinuhe, Isis,' said Sheri. 'Then hurry upstairs and get yourself ready. It's almost time to leave.'

Isis took the fish stew and bread through to the front room, peering inside before entering. Sinuhe was lying down, staring blankly at the wall, and the room was full of his earthy odour. Isis felt it catch in her throat. She placed the bowl before him. Sinuhe said nothing. Isis watched as he sat upright and reached for the bread. He tore it in two with his big, rough hands, and dipped one half in the stew. He didn't even look at Isis.

'Isis!' Kia's voice drifted down the stairs. 'Hurry up!'

She turned and skipped away, but the image of those gnarled, grubby hands stuck in her mind as she prepared her own smooth body for the evening's dancing. Kia covered her in sweet-smelling oils and placed a short, neat wig on her head. Isis adjusted it, peering into the bronze mirror that Sheri held for her.

Then she reached for a band of beads that fitted over the wig, adding a splash of colour, and for another band to sling around her waist.

'Just your make-up and you'll be done,' said Sheri. 'We need to hurry. We're going to be late.'

Isis turned to Mut, who was sitting with the pots of kohl and red ochre. The two girls always did each other's make-up, so it felt very strange not to be doing Mut's. Mut wasn't even coming; she was going to stay behind with Hopi, Ramose and Kha – and Sinuhe, of course. Isis sat still, and closed her eyes to let her dance partner encircle them with the black kohl eyeliner, then sucked in her cheeks as Mut brushed on a little red ochre powder.

'I'm dreading this,' Isis whispered.

'Sorry, Isis,' murmured Mut. 'But you'll be fine without me. Just think – I have to stay in the house with *him*. The boys are scared he'll put mice in their beds.'

Isis grinned, in spite of herself. Then she let out a long, slow breath. She'd be glad when the night was over.

'Everybody ready?' called Paneb's voice from down the stairs.

Isis reached for her linen shawl and slung it around her shoulders. Nefert appeared in the doorway in her beautiful white performance gown, made of linen so fine you could almost see through it.

'See you later,' muttered Isis.

The mansion of Abana the tax collector was on the road towards the great temples of Ipet-Isut, where many of Waset's most gracious homes were situated. The troupe was met at the gate by guards, who ushered them through lush gardens lit up with oil lamps, and guided them to the back of the house. There, servants led them past a courtyard where vast amounts of food and drink were being prepared, then into a little room, where the women removed their shawls and checked their make-up.

'Well, he's certainly rich,' commented Nefert. 'This is one of the biggest mansions we've ever visited.'

'Newly rich.' Kia sniffed. 'Look at all this new furniture – far too much of it everywhere. The man has no taste at all.'

Isis was feeling too nervous to take much notice. She wished that Hopi had come, but he didn't join the troupe at parties in Waset; there was no need. A servant led them into a banqueting hall, where the richest men and women of the town were already milling around, admiring each other's wigs and sipping wine. Isis wondered which man was Abana.

Usually, the host came to talk to the troupe personally, but they had only met servants and guards so far.

A male servant told them to start playing, and Isis tried to relax. She felt exposed without Mut. It was strange – almost as though her dance partner gave her a kind of shield. She stuck to old routines, ones that she could do without thinking. Gradually, the guests began to sit down and watch. But she still had no idea who the host was.

The troupe played and danced until the servant said they could stop for a break. He led them back to the same little room, where they were served grapes, figs, slices of melon and beakers of beer.

Paneb seemed preoccupied, almost angry. 'How am I supposed to approach Abana when I don't even know who he is?' he demanded.

'We can always enquire once we've finished,' said Sheri.

'He'll be drunk by then.' Paneb spat out a grape pip. 'Then what am I going to tell Sinuhe?'

He paced up and down in a fury. Isis watched him, baffled. She still didn't understand why Paneb was so bothered about Sinuhe. She thought of the peasant's rough hands and rougher manners. The longer he stayed in their house, the less she liked him.

'Brother, you must not worry about your cousin

too much,' said Kia. 'After all, his misfortunes are not your fault. We can do only so much to help.'

'Only so much!' Paneb glared at his sister-in-law. 'Kia, you don't know what you're saying. I *must* speak with Abana before the end of the evening.'

The servant returned to take them back to the banqueting hall. The guests were more boisterous now, and many of the women were drunk. Isis felt everyone's eyes on her as she danced.

Not long now, she kept telling herself, *not long . . .*

One man in particular seemed to be watching her closely and, as she gave her final bow, he beckoned her over.

Isis glanced anxiously at Nefert, who put down her lute.

'I'll come with you, Isis,' she said.

They walked over and stood in front of the man, who was surrounded by a group of friends. Isis bowed her head as she reached him.

'At your service, sir.'

The man looked at Nefert. 'A fine dancer you have,' he commented. 'She's exquisite. I hired you on a recommendation, and I haven't been disappointed.'

Isis gave a start. So *this* was Abana!

'We are happy to hear that, sir,' responded Nefert.

'I should like to see her again,' said Abana.

'Well,' said Nefert cautiously, 'we are very busy at the moment in the run-up to the Beautiful Festival of the Valley, as I'm sure you can understand.'

'Every night?' snapped Abana. 'I find that hard to believe. Anyway, I don't want all of you. I just want to see this dancer again.'

Isis felt her heart beating faster. All her instincts told her that this man couldn't be trusted – and the thought of dancing alone again filled her with horror. She waited for Nefert to speak up in her defence, but her guardian's next words came as a shock.

'If you're so pleased with our performance, perhaps you would consider doing us a favour,' said Nefert. 'There's something my husband wishes to discuss with you.'

The tax collector narrowed his eyes, and a cynical smile twitched at the corner of his mouth. 'A favour, indeed!' he exclaimed. 'But you haven't given me an answer.'

'If you would just listen to my husband,' said Nefert.

Isis couldn't believe it. Nefert was *trading* her – trading her on behalf of Sinuhe! She felt panic rising and turned to Nefert. 'But I don't –'

'Hush, Isis. I know.' Nefert silenced her with a glare.

Abana grinned. He was surrounded by even more guests now, all wanting his attention, while two of the servants hovered nearby. He stood and dismissed Nefert with a wave of his hand. 'Tell your husband to do *me* a favour,' he said. 'I want to see this dancer tomorrow, and I won't listen to anything unless he agrees to my terms. Is that clear?'

CHAPTER FOUR

The house was quiet. Mut, Ramose and Kha were asleep, curled up together on mats in the back room. Hopi had returned home just before the troupe left for Abana's party. Once they had gone, he had served himself the remains of the fish stew and carried it up on to the roof, where he mopped it up with chunks of bread. Then he laid the bowl down and watched the sun set over the western mountains, thinking.

He had learned a lot that day. He thought about the scarabs, with their perfect balls of dung. He thought of Khepri, the scarab god of the rising sun, and imagined him pushing the sun up out of the underworld every morning.

Then he thought of the peasant and his stories about Abana. Right now, his own family was performing in that villain's house. Hopi felt anger rising

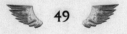

again. Farmers' lives were difficult enough – they toiled under the hot sun for most of the year, and when they had finished sowing, they were put to work on the king's building projects, or made to repair the irrigation canals. Unscrupulous tax collectors had no right to make their lives any harder! The injustice of it made Hopi clench his fists in fury.

It was dark now, the bulk of the mountains only just visible against the western sky. Twinkling oil lamps lit the homes of Waset, giving a faint glow to the town. Hopi got to his feet and limped across the roof with his bowl.

'Boy.'

Hopi jumped. He peered down the stairs, and could just make out Sinuhe standing at the bottom. His heart swelled, thinking of how the peasant had suffered. 'Can I get anything for you?' he asked.

'I wish to speak with you.' Sinuhe's voice was grave.

'Of course. I'll just put this in the courtyard.'

Hopi made his way down the stairs and out to the back of the house. The peasant followed him, staying close as Hopi tipped some water into the empty bowl. He lit an oil lamp and carried it through to the front room with Sinuhe still at his heels.

'Who are you?' demanded Sinuhe, as soon as they had sat down.

Hopi was taken aback. 'Who? I'm Hopi.'

'I've heard your name spoken already,' said the peasant. 'What I mean is this: who *are* you? What are you doing in this house?'

Hopi stared at him for a moment. This wasn't what he'd been expecting. 'I'm the brother of Isis,' he said eventually. 'Isis is a dancer. She works with the troupe alongside Paneb's daughter Mut.'

Sinuhe ignored this information. 'I see how you steal from my cousin.'

Hopi's mouth dropped open. *'Steal?'* he echoed. 'What are you talking about?'

'I see how you help yourself to food.' The peasant's eyes were flashing; he seemed genuinely angry. Hopi wasn't sure how to react.

'I live here,' he said. 'I'm allowed to help myself to food. If you think I make no contribution –'

'I think you're a lazy good-for-nothing. I see how you come and go as you please. I see how you spend your days in idleness. I see what you are.' Sinuhe's lips became flecked with foam as he spat his words out at Hopi.

Hopi sat very still. The peasant was clearly raving, but his words were frightening, too.

Stay calm, he told himself. *He's just a poor peasant.*

'I . . . I bring . . .' The words came out weak and

quavery, and he had to clear his throat. 'I bring an income to this house, sir,' he carried on. Saying it out loud made him braver. 'It's not very much yet, but it will be more when I've finished my apprenticeship. I'm a trainee priest of Serqet and the people of Waset reward me for what I do.'

But Sinuhe wasn't listening. 'He never understood hardship,' he mumbled. He folded his gnarled hands together. 'I knew this was what I would find. Waste and idleness. Decadence and ruin . . .'

Hopi decided he'd had enough. He had wanted to help this man, and instead he was listening to insults. He got up and left the room, leaving the oil lamp to Sinuhe.

Isis woke to the sound of voices. Nefert . . . Paneb . . . Sheri, perhaps . . . the voices rose and fell. Then they grew louder, and she opened her eyes. Morning light was filtering into the room.

'I don't think it's fair on her.' That was Sheri.

'She managed perfectly well last night,' responded Paneb. 'We wouldn't ask her to do it otherwise. I don't like to make her work against her will, but this problem lies heavily upon me, Sheri. It will do her no harm.'

With a start, Isis realised that the adults were

talking about *her*. She lay stiffly under her linen cover, listening.

'But there are other ways,' insisted Sheri. 'This problem is between you and your cousin. It has nothing to do with Isis. It isn't right to make use of her like this.'

'Sister, you don't understand –'

'If I *was* your sister, I might,' Sheri snapped back. 'But as your sister-in-law, I can't even be sure he is kin.'

Paneb fell silent. Isis rolled on her side and peeped out from under her sheet. The three adults were at the top of the steps on the roof, their voices drifting down to where she lay. She threw back the cover and sat up. Mut and the boys were nowhere to be seen; they must be down in the courtyard already. Isis crept closer to the steps.

'I wish I could explain,' said Paneb. 'But all I can say is that there's no doubt. He is my cousin, and I am obliged to help him.'

'Very well,' said Sheri. 'We can give him some grain. But what more can he possibly expect after all these years?'

Paneb gave a heavy sigh. 'I'm afraid it's not quite so simple,' he said. 'A gift of grain will not be enough to satisfy him. He has vowed to remain here until

I fulfil my responsibilities.'

'*Fulfil your responsibilities?*' Now it was Nefert's turn to sound incredulous. 'Whatever is that supposed to mean? You haven't told me this, Paneb.'

'Sinuhe spoke to me this morning,' said Paneb.

Isis tiptoed a little further up the steps. Now she could just see the three adults sitting cross-legged on the roof.

'And what did he say?' demanded Nefert.

'He pointed out that we support strangers: we give them shelter and food. He says that if we can do that, we should do more to support our own kin.'

'Support *strangers*?' exclaimed Sheri.

'Hopi and Isis.'

Isis caught her breath.

'But Isis *works* for us,' protested Sheri. 'She earns her keep, and she wouldn't be here without Hopi. Even Hopi brings us all he can.'

'*I* know that,' said Paneb. 'But it is not so straightforward in the eyes of my cousin. The ties of blood run deep, Sheri. I have to do my best by Sinuhe. Surely you can see that?'

With a sinking heart, Isis realised the truth. For some reason, Paneb had to prove his loyalty to Sinuhe. He had to show that his cousin meant as much as the 'strangers' who lived under his roof. And that meant one thing: Isis would have to return to the tax collector's house to perform that evening.

When Hopi arrived at Menna's house, the old man was sitting in a patch of morning sun in the courtyard, his eyes closed. Hopi approached him softly.

'Good morning, Menna.'

Menna looked up. 'Hopi. I've been expecting you.'

Hopi sat down next to his tutor. 'I did as you told me to yesterday,' he said. 'I went out into the fields to find some scarabs.'

A little smile curled Menna's lips. 'I hope you enjoyed yourself.'

'Well, it was interesting.'

'Tell me what you saw.' Menna closed his eyes again, waiting for Hopi to speak.

Hopi thought for a moment. He watched the sunlight play over the old man's skin, taking in the lines like birds' feet that surrounded his eyes, the deep hollows under his cheekbones, the ridges that furrowed his brow. He remembered what Menna had said on his way to the family tomb: *there are some lessons that only the gods can teach* . . . Did these words have anything to do with scarabs?

Menna opened one eye and raised an eyebrow. 'Well?' he asked.

Hopi came out of his reverie. He described all that he had seen: the mound of donkey dung, the scurrying scarabs, their perfect spheres and their journey to their burrows. When he had finished, Menna nodded slowly.

'Very good,' he said. 'Very good. You've seen the first half of the cycle. But it seems you did not see the second.'

'The second?' Hopi was puzzled.

Menna reached for the little casket that was sitting by his side – the same one that he had opened the day before. 'The first half of the scarab's cycle shows dedication and labour. In the second half, the hard work is over,' Menna told him. 'All that remains is magic.'

Hopi thought back to the scarabs. He hadn't seen anything very magical about them. 'No, I don't think I saw that,' he said honestly.

'No matter. You will, all in good time.'

Menna lifted the lid of the casket. He brought out the blue faience scarab again and placed it on the mat in front of him. But he didn't stop there. Next he fetched out an *ankh*, the symbol of life. Then there was another scarab, an *udjat* eye of Horus, a *djed* pillar, more *udjat* eyes . . . slowly, methodically, he laid them all out until there were twenty-nine amulets spread before them. He reached into the casket one last time and brought out a beautiful scarab of green jasper set in a thin casing of gold, which he set to one side, apart from all the others.

'These are my brother's funerary amulets,' he said. 'They must be placed among his wrappings.' He picked up the jasper scarab and turned it over to reveal hieroglyphs carved into the gold. 'This is his heart scarab, inscribed with a text from the *Book of the Dead*. It is the most important amulet of all, to be placed over his heart.'

Hopi stared at the array of amulets in front of him. He had never been so close to the secrets of the dead before. 'When will that be?' he asked. 'Don't the embalmers need them?'

'Indeed they do,' said Menna. 'And that is where you come in. I want you to deliver them for me. You must take them to the embalmers' workshops.'

Hopi's heart leaped. The workshops were shrouded in secrecy; few people could afford to have their relatives embalmed, and the process their bodies went through was shrouded in magic and ritual. He knew he was being granted a great privilege.

'Thank you, Menna,' he said.

Menna began putting the amulets back into the casket. 'But I have one condition. You must complete your studies of the scarab, for it is the scarab that protects the heart.'

'Willingly,' breathed Hopi.

The old priest reached for his stick. With an effort, he got to his feet, and picked up the casket. 'Now we must make an offering. The amulets must be blessed, and so must you. Only then will you be fit to be the bearer of such power. Come.'

Hopi followed his tutor inside the house. They entered a cool, dim room, where a shrine to the goddess Serqet stood in one corner. All around were the tools of Menna's trade: strings of onions, herbs, bottles of oil, pieces of dried-out dung.

'We must make our offering to Anubis,' said Menna. He brought out a little statue of the jackal-headed god and placed it next to Serqet on her shrine. 'Kneel down here, Hopi. Let's pour the god a libation of sweet oil.'

As Hopi kneeled in front of the shrine, Menna fetched a jug of fragranced oil and poured some in front of the statue, murmuring a prayer. He lifted the casket of amulets on to a table nearby. Hopi glanced up and saw that he was transferring them into a smaller wooden box, wrapping each one in scraps of linen for padding. He placed the box on the shrine, murmured more prayers and poured another libation.

'Now may the gods bless Hopi, he who will be their bearer,' he intoned, placing his hand on Hopi's head. Then he reached for the box and placed it in Hopi's hands. 'These amulets are now in your care,' he said. 'Do not open the box or touch them, for they are destined for the Kingdom of the Dead. Give them only to the chief embalmer Weni. Go early tomorrow. Is that clear?'

Mut listened to the news, then jutted out her lip in disappointment. 'You mean, you'll be going back to Abana's without me?'

'I don't *want* to do it, Mut!' cried Isis. 'I wish you could come with me.'

'But why does he want you to go back alone?' persisted Mut. 'I don't get it, Isis. Why can't he wait until it's the two of us?'

Isis shrugged. 'How should I know?'

'I'm just as pretty as you,' said Mut.

'You weren't even there,' snapped Isis. 'He doesn't know whether you're pretty or not. He doesn't even know who you *are*.'

She got to her feet and ran up to the roof feeling furious. Mut was impossible when she was in this kind of mood. It was bad enough returning to Abana without her dance partner making life difficult as well. Sometimes she hated living in this house – however hard she and Hopi worked, they would never truly belong. Mut didn't know how lucky she was.

She paced across the rooftop, waiting for Hopi. She wanted to tell her brother everything. Maybe – just maybe – he would think of a way out of it. At last she spotted him, limping along the street.

'Hopi!' she called. 'Come up here!'

The minute her brother appeared at the top of the stairs, she catapulted herself into his arms.

'You've got to help me! Come and sit. Here, put your bag down –'

'No!' Hopi snatched his bag out of Isis's grasp. 'Stop it!'

Isis stopped in surprise. 'I was only getting you to sit.' She peered at Hopi's bag. 'What have you got in there? A snake?'

'No, I haven't got a snake.' Hopi lowered himself on to the mats. 'You should just be more careful, that's all. Now, what's wrong?'

Isis eyed the bag curiously. She knew Hopi too well. There *was* something interesting inside it, she was sure, but she'd find out soon enough what it was. She poured out her story, describing Abana's party and everything she'd heard about Sinuhe.

'It's all Sinuhe's fault,' she finished. 'It's all because of him that I have to go back to Abana's. I don't want to, Hopi. I hate dancing without Mut.'

Hopi's face clouded with anger. 'Abana's a monster,' he said. 'Paneb and Nefert shouldn't make you go.'

'Nefert and Sheri stood up for me, but Sinuhe has Paneb wrapped around his little finger.' Isis shuddered. 'It's horrible, having him creep around the house.'

'Something's not right.' Hopi frowned. 'I feel sorry for Sinuhe, but there's more to his troubles than meets the eye. All the same, I believe his story. He's not the only peasant to suffer at the hands of Abana.'

'You've heard of others?'

'Yes.' Hopi nodded. 'I heard another story out in the fields only yesterday.'

'What were you doing there?' demanded Isis. She glanced at his bag again. 'I thought you were at Menna's. It's got something to do with your bag, hasn't it? What are you hiding, Hopi?'

Hopi relented. 'All right, Isis, I'll tell you. Menna sent me out to study the life of sacred scarabs, so I had to go and find some. I still don't understand why, not really. Anyway, today he's given me his brother's funerary amulets. There's a green jasper scarab to be placed on his heart. It's amazing – it's cased in gold. I have to take them all to the embalmers' workshops tomorrow.'

'Amulets!' Isis felt a rush of pride for her brother, and also a ripple of fear. Funerary amulets were very powerful – full of magic. 'You have them here?'

Hopi nodded. 'They're in my bag.'

Isis gazed at it with a new respect. 'How many are there?'

'About thirty.'

'Thirty!'

'That's the usual number, Isis.'

'I know, but . . .' Isis shook her head. The thought of there being so much magic in her brother's bag was unsettling somehow. She badly wanted to see them, but she didn't dare ask. 'I can't believe they're just sitting there.'

'I know. Well, they won't be for long.' Hopi drew the bag closer to his side. 'And first, we have to sort out this business about Abana. When do you have to go back?'

'Tonight,' said Isis.

'I can't do much about that,' said Hopi. 'But there's one thing I can do. You don't have to go alone, Isis. I'm coming with you, and nobody's going to stop me.'

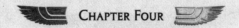

Isis felt so relieved that she barely noticed the movement at the top of the stairs. But about an hour later, as Mut helped her with her make-up, she remembered it. There had been someone there while she was talking to Hopi, someone who'd ducked down as she'd turned her head. Suddenly, it was clear. It had been Sinuhe, listening to every word.

CHAPTER FIVE

'Hurry up, Hopi. You can walk faster than that.'

Nefert's voice was sharp, and Hopi bristled. It wasn't his fault that he had a limp.

Isis shot him a nervous, sympathetic smile. 'We're almost there,' she whispered, and pointed out the large, imposing gateway that led to Abana's mansion.

Nefert knocked, and a guard opened the gate just a crack, holding an oil lamp.

'Who are you?' he demanded.

'We're Abana's performers,' responded Nefert. 'He's expecting us.'

The guard peered at them, moving his lamp around to give them a good once-over. 'I was told one girl was coming,' he said. 'No one else has been authorised.'

'Oh, but that's absurd!' exclaimed Nefert. 'She's young. I can't possibly allow her in alone. Besides, she needs some music. I play the lute.' And she showed her instrument, which was slung over her shoulder.

The guard looked dubious. 'Suppose that makes sense,' he said grudgingly. He nodded at Hopi. 'What about him?'

'I'm her brother,' said Hopi. 'I've come to look after her.'

The guard snorted, and Hopi bit his lip. He should have known that a guard would want better reasons than that.

'She'll be looked after all right here.' The guard cast an eye at the scars on Hopi's leg. 'Don't look like you're much use to her, anyway.'

'How dare –' began Hopi.

'Hush.' Nefert silenced him with a glance. 'Very well. I shall accompany Isis inside.' She turned to Hopi. 'I'm sorry, Hopi, but I'll see that no harm comes to her. You may as well go home.'

The guard opened the gate wider to allow Nefert and Isis inside. He grinned at Hopi. 'Sorry, *brother*. Better luck next time,' he said, and banged the gate shut.

Hopi was furious. He thumped the gate with his

fist. Then he turned and leaned against it, thinking fast. He wasn't going to leave now, whatever the guard might say.

The road was deserted. Hopi began to walk along the boundary wall, examining it closely. It was made of mud brick smoothed over with plaster. Here and there, the plaster had broken off to reveal the brick-work beneath. In the moonlight, he hunted for a piece of stone, then found a section where acacia bushes grew close to the wall. He began work, chipping through the plaster to make footholds. He looked up. The wall wasn't so very high. As long as the guards didn't patrol the wall too often, he should be all right.

Hitching his bag over his shoulder, he began to climb. He peered over the top into the grounds and saw that the house was hidden behind trees. There were no signs of any guards. Feeling more courageous, he hooked one leg up over the top of the wall and dropped down on the other side. Thinking ahead, he found another stone and began making footholds for his escape. He was much more exposed now, conscious of every little scrape and tap.

Voices.

Hopi flattened himself against the wall, and froze. There was nowhere to hide.

Two men were walking through the grounds, deep in discussion. They hadn't seen Hopi. He dived behind a tree, listening.

'. . . can't get back any faster,' one man was saying.

'You could if you . . .' Hopi missed the end of the sentence.

'But then I'd lose the contract.' The first man seemed frustrated and angry.

'Yes. Well, maybe. But that's why I've brought you here. I want you to see what a big shipment you'd be losing if you refuse,' said the second man.

They moved down the pathway, and Hopi could hear no more. But they were walking away from the mansion, not towards it. Hopi's curiosity got the better of him. What shipment was the man talking about? And where were they going? Slipping from tree to tree, he began to follow.

Beyond the gardens, there was a dense grove of fig trees that seemed to stretch right to the edge of the grounds. But as he made his way through it, Hopi could see that it ended sooner than he'd thought. There was an open area up ahead with a building positioned at the centre. Hopi was just in time to spot the two men disappearing into it.

Hopi waited in the shadows of the fig trees for the men to return. They soon reappeared, and he managed to catch a glimpse of their faces in the moonlight as they passed, walking back towards the house. They were silent now, preoccupied. When all was quiet, Hopi crept towards the building, circling it until he saw an entrance. It certainly wasn't a house – it had no windows and only one door. Hopi pushed it, then pulled it. It was shut fast. He put his eye up to chinks in the planks, but he couldn't see anything in the darkness.

Then he noticed. On the ground leading up to the entrance, there were clues. Hopi bent down and scooped up half a handful of something that lay scattered around. He fingered and sniffed it. It was grain.

As Hopi gazed up at the building, his heart filled with anger. This store was enormous – enough to feed half the town. It wasn't difficult to work out what the tax collector was up to. This wasn't a government granary, but Abana's stolen grain. The man must be exposed, but how? Abana was head of all Waset's tax collectors; he answered only to the highest men in the land.

A jackal howled in the distance, out towards the desert. Hopi realised that it was getting late. He

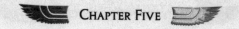
would have to think about his discovery later – if he didn't hurry, he might miss seeing Isis dance altogether.

The house seemed very different without all its guests. The rooms were badly lit, with many in darkness. A servant holding a single oil lamp showed Isis and Nefert into a shadowy chamber, where they found Abana sitting alone, eating a leg of goose. Isis felt her stomach lurch with nerves.

Nefert sat down with her lute and began to play. Abana ripped at the goose flesh with his teeth until Isis started to dance. Then he paused, still gripping the leg bone, to stare at her. Isis knew she was dancing badly. It was very difficult performing on her own with him looking at her like that. Her legs felt stiff and heavy, her movements clumsy. But Abana didn't seem to mind. He finished the goose leg without taking his eyes off her, then slammed the bone down on to his plate.

'Stop!'

Isis was mid-pirouette, but did as he said, her arms still up in the air. Nefert stopped plucking the strings of the lute.

'What is it, sir?' asked Nefert. 'Are we not pleasing you?'

'I told you it was just the girl I wanted. I didn't ask for music.'

'But she can't dance without music,' Nefert pointed out.

'Nonsense.' Abana stood and walked towards Isis. He grasped her by the shoulders, his fingers still oily with goose fat. She tried not to shudder.

'Let her go.' Nefert's voice was sharp.

Abana grinned. 'Dance, girl,' he instructed Isis.

Isis threw a frightened glance at Nefert. To her relief, her guardian stood up, her features stern.

'Let her *go!*' Nefert shouted.

Abana released Isis with a shove that sent her spinning. She gasped, nearly fell, then managed to regain her balance.

Her eyes flashing, Nefert stepped between Isis and Abana. 'That's enough!' she said. 'Such behaviour is unacceptable. We shall leave immediately.'

The tax collector gave a cynical smile, and strolled back to his table to pick up the goose bone. 'If you leave, I shall pay you nothing,' he said, with his back turned.

'That matters little to us.' Isis couldn't be sure, but she thought that Nefert's voice shook.

'Is that so? And what about the favour you wanted to ask?' Abana queried. He turned around and looked at them with mocking eyes, sucking on the bone.

Isis saw Nefert hesitate, just for a second. But then her guardian raised her chin and spoke haughtily. 'There are no favours that we wish to ask of you.' She picked up her lute. 'Come, Isis. We must go.'

Thankfully, Isis placed her hand in Nefert's, and they hurried out of the room. A servant pointed them in the direction of the gate.

'That was quick, hey?' commented the guard, his tone insolent.

Nefert gripped Isis's hand a little tighter. 'Let us out, please.'

The guard grinned, and shoved the gate open. 'Dare say that brother will be pleased to see you,' he sneered.

Hopi had reached the walls of the mansion, but it was impossible to see inside. There was an open veranda, but it was deserted; doors to the inner chambers were all shut. There were only clerestory windows, high up towards the roof. Hopi had been sure there would be some way to spy on Abana, but if there was one, he couldn't see it.

He made his way around the house, listening for the sound of Nefert's lute. Servants' voices drifted out from somewhere deep inside, but that was all. Hopi edged carefully to the veranda, wondering if there was some way he could break in. The voices drew closer, and Hopi froze.

'What was that?' he heard.

'What?'

'I saw something moving in the shadows there . . .'

He'd been spotted. His heart thumping, Hopi backed away from the veranda, then tore through the gardens to the place where he'd climbed the wall. With a surge of energy, he leaped at it, bounding up with a strength he didn't know he possessed. Wriggling to the top, he threw one leg over, then hurled his body after it. He landed badly, crashing on to the ground, and almost yelped in pain.

But he couldn't stop. He scrambled to his feet. Wincing with every step, he half-ran, half-hobbled up the road and dived behind a limestone statue that stood at the entrance to the next house. Gasping for breath, he peered around it. The guards had come out and were staring up the road. One of them approached, and Hopi ducked back, trying to quieten his breathing. The guard stopped before reaching him, calling back to his companion.

'Can't see anything here.'

'Leave it, then. Could have been a jackal.'

Hopi closed his eyes in relief as the guard's steps

retreated back to the gate. He shifted his weight, trying to breathe through his nose. Agonising pains were shooting up his bad leg. He rubbed it, wondering whether to wait for Isis. He had no idea how long he had spent digging footholds in the wall, or investigating the grain store. Perhaps she had already left. Eventually he could bear the uncertainty no longer. Limping heavily, he began to hobble home.

Nefert was silent as they made their way back through the streets of Waset. Isis could still feel her anger smouldering beneath her tight-lipped features. She was intensely grateful that her guardian had defended her so fiercely, but she longed to speak to Hopi. The moment they arrived back, she ran through the house looking for him. Sinuhe was in the front room. Sheri, Kia, Mut and the boys were up on the roof. But her brother was nowhere to be seen.

She ran down from the roof, past the first-floor practice room, and stopped. She could hear angry voices.

'You just walked out?' Paneb sounded incredulous.

'*Of course* we walked out.' Nefert was clearly still furious.

'She's old enough to cope with a bit of solo dancing.'

'Not for a man like that! I won't stand for it, Paneb.

Just think if it had been Mut.' Nefert's voice shook with rage. Isis felt relieved; she knew now that Nefert would defend her to the end.

'We have to find a solution to this.' There was something desperate in Paneb's tone.

'He's your cousin – *you* find a solution! As if I don't feel betrayed enough.' Nefert quavered as though she were close to tears.

'How have I ever betrayed you?' It was Paneb's turn to sound outraged. 'I've been constant for all these years, I've found the troupe work and success beyond your wildest hopes.'

'You lied to me from the outset! You are not what you seem.' Nefert was clearly crying now.

Paneb seemed to think for a moment. 'Is it so terrible that my cousin is a peasant?' he asked. His voice was quieter, but there was no more warmth in it. He seemed hard and distant.

Isis was horrified. She had heard Nefert and Paneb quarrel before, but never like this. And it was all because of Sinuhe. How had one man managed to create such havoc in their household?

'I no longer care who he is, or what he's doing here,' said Nefert. 'I just want him to leave.'

'He says the gods have sent him,' said Paneb. 'He was given a sign.'

'And you're content to listen to the riddles of a simpleton!' shouted Nefert. 'Sort it out, Paneb, or who knows what will befall us!'

Isis couldn't bear to hear any more. She slipped back down to the courtyard and sat there in the dark, the words of the argument rattling around her head. What a dreadful evening it had been . . . she could still feel the oily grip of Abana's hands on her shoulders, and see the mockery in his eyes when they'd left. She wanted very badly to talk to Hopi.

'Isis.'

She looked up, and saw her brother standing in the doorway to the courtyard. 'Hopi! There you are!' Isis got up and rushed into his arms.

Hopi hopped over the threshold. 'Isis, you're back already . . . Ow!' He grimaced as he put his foot down.

'You're hurt!' exclaimed Isis. 'What happened?'

'I was trying to escape,' said Hopi. He told her about the grain store he had found, and how he had almost been caught. 'I fell as I landed,' he finished. 'It's nothing – I'll be all right. I just need some of Mut's balm.'

'I'll get it.' Isis ran to fetch it, then squatted down next to him, dipping her fingers in the balm. 'There. Does that help?'

'Ow,' Hopi winced as Isis rubbed a bit too hard. 'Yes, a bit. So why are you back so early? What happened?'

In a low voice, Isis described everything that had happened, from her horrible evening with Abana to the row between Nefert and Paneb. As she expected, Hopi was furious about the tax collector.

'We'll pay him back, Isis. We will,' he vowed.

Isis finished dabbing the balm, and looked up. 'It's fine. Nefert stood up for me and we left straight away.' She sighed. 'I'm more worried about her row with Paneb. Sinuhe is causing us a lot of problems, Hopi.'

Hopi nodded. 'We'll soon work out why, Isis,' he promised. 'Once I've delivered Menna's amulets, I'll make it my business to find out.'

CHAPTER SIX

In spite of his painful leg, Hopi was determined to make Menna's delivery as quickly as possible the next morning. The workshops were towards the temples of Ipet-Isut, not far from the grand houses of people like Abana; the difference was that they were hidden away along the riverbank, out of public view. Embalming was a gruesome business, and people didn't like getting too close to it.

Towering palm trees marked the site of the workshops, and Hopi hobbled to the entrance. He found a pair of guards half asleep under a tree, and shook one of them awake.

'I have a delivery,' Hopi told him. 'I'm the apprentice of Menna, priest of Serqet. He has sent a letter for the head embalmer.' He delved into his bag and brought out a little papyrus scroll.

The guard rubbed his eyes. 'Can't read,' he mumbled, then nudged his colleague. 'Go and get one of the embalmers. Boy says he's got a delivery.'

The second guard sleepily got to his feet, and set off towards one of the tents that Hopi could just see between the trees. When he returned, it was with a man whose kilt and hands were stained with dried blood.

'I am an assistant embalmer. Do you have authorisation to be here?' the man enquired. Hopi showed him the papyrus scroll. The assistant inspected it and nodded. 'You are welcome, apprentice of Menna,' he said. 'I'll take you to Weni, the chief embalmer. Follow me.'

Hopi set off after him, curiosity burning. He had always wanted to see this place. Up ahead were three tents. As the assistant led him past the first one, Hopi peered back at it, wondering what was inside.

The assistant spotted his interest and smiled. 'That's where we wash the bodies when they first arrive,' he explained, and carried on towards the second. 'This tent is where we prepare them for drying and cover them in natron.'

He pushed back a flap and entered. Hopi followed him eagerly, not sure what to expect – and immediately got a surprise. The first thing that hit him was the smell: the heavy stench of dead flesh, thick and choking. The tent was spacious enough – designed, no doubt, so that fresh air could circulate – but nothing could mask that horrible odour. Hopi felt his stomach turn.

The assistant led the way past mounds of natron salt and a stack of canopic jars. Hopi stared at the mounds. They were body-shaped. There were dead people lying buried in the salt, slowly drying out.

'Hmm. I thought Weni was doing his inspection here,' said the assistant. 'No matter. He must be in the next tent. That's where the bodies are wrapped.'

Hopi followed him to the final tent. If possible, the smell here was even stronger, but at least it was easier to bear. The tent was filled with vats of different oils and resins, perfumes and spices, all used to anoint the bodies as they were wrapped. In one corner stood a huge pile of ready-woven linen; a boy sat cross-legged, cutting it into strips. Two men were examining a fully wrapped body laid out on the table. The assistant approached them.

'This boy has come with amulets from Menna,' he said.

'Ah, good,' said one of the men. He stepped away from the body and greeted Hopi. 'I am Weni, the chief embalmer. And this is Hetep, the lector priest, who sanctifies all that happens here.'

'I am honoured to meet you.' Hopi fetched out Menna's wooden box. 'These are the amulets.'

Weni accepted the box and handed it to Hetep. They both closed their eyes for a second. Hopi stared at them, then saw that Hetep's lips were moving. The lector priest was murmuring a spell. With the box in the palm of one hand, he moved the other to hover over it, and began chanting the spell more loudly. Hopi felt awed and incredibly lucky to witness something so sacred.

The spell came to an end. 'May the gods judge his heart light and free of burden,' Hetep finished, and opened his eyes.

'There. Thank you, Hopi. Your task is done.' Weni took the box from the priest's hands, then disappeared behind a linen curtain that Hopi hadn't noticed before. As the fabric swung to one side, he caught a glimpse of an area crammed with statues, caskets and coffins. A mask of Anubis seemed to look straight at him and, instinctively, he took a step back. This was a holy place.

Weni emerged from behind the curtain. 'I will escort you back to the entrance,' he said. 'Come.'

Hopi walked out into the sunshine. It was a relief; the air had been hot and oppressive inside. He glanced towards the river and saw that a man was walking up from the jetty. Weni saw him, too, and stopped.

'You have better news for me this time, I hope?' said the embalmer.

The man looked embarrassed. 'I'm leaving the day after tomorrow,' he said.

'That's very late. You should be leaving sooner,' said Weni, clearly frustrated. 'So when will you return?'

The man shifted from one foot to the other. 'I can't say. The river is unpredictable . . .'

Hopi stared at him. His face was oddly familiar.

'That's strange,' said Weni, his voice hard. 'It was perfectly reliable before.'

'Yes, yes, indeed it is strange.' The man nodded.

'And you're a liar,' said the embalmer. 'I want to make one thing clear: if we don't receive a shipment of natron by the end of next week, I shall seek another supplier. Do you understand?'

At the mention of the word *shipment*, something slipped into place. Of course: this was one of the men that Hopi had seen in the grounds of Abana's mansion only the night before.

'But –' began the man.

'No buts. My word on this is final,' snapped Weni.

'I understand,' said the man. 'You will receive your

natron, Weni.' He turned and walked back towards the Nile, his head bowed.

Weni watched him go, his face clouded with anger. 'We cannot work without natron,' he said. 'This man is holding us to ransom.'

Hopi was intrigued. 'I'm sorry to hear it.'

Weni shook his head. 'Meanwhile, we must suffer this loathsome stench.'

'You mean, it's not usually like this?' Hopi asked.

'There's always a certain odour,' admitted Weni. 'But it's worse at the moment because we can't use a deeper layer of natron. The bodies are barely covered. Some . . .' He shook his head, then spoke more briskly. 'Well, that's not your concern. I must take you to the entrance.'

Weni marched purposefully through the second tent. Hopi darted glances to the left and right, sizing up the bodies that lay on either side of him. Now that Weni had pointed it out, he could make out their forms more easily than he might have expected. Hopi set out for Menna's house, his thoughts buzzing.

The atmosphere was tense. Mut and Isis sat playing with Ramose and Kha at the far end of the courtyard, keeping the two boys out of the adults' way. After their row the night before, Paneb and Nefert were barely speaking to each other; Paneb stayed on the roof, Nefert on the first floor, while Sheri and Kia performed the household chores methodically.

'I'm getting tired of slaving for this cousin of ours.' Kia spoke almost under her breath, as she stirred a pot of lentil soup.

Isis knew she wasn't meant to hear. She carried on weaving a straw man for Kha, careful not to look over at Kia. But she did sneak a look at Mut, and saw that her dance partner was listening, too.

'It can't be for much longer.' Sheri was pummelling a fresh batch of dough.

'I'm not so sure. Now that we've failed with Abana, we'll never get rid of him.'

Sheri sighed. 'I agree it would help if he was a little more grateful for what we do.'

'Grateful!' Kia snorted. 'He doesn't know the meaning of the word. Never says a word of thanks for the food we serve, never smiles. Treats us like servants, or worse.'

'I know. But we have to make allowances, Kia. After all he's been through –'

'Make allowances!' Kia was working herself into a rage. 'I don't see why. He's shown up here, claiming he's kin, taking every last scrap he's given and more. How do we know who he is? He's –'

'I know, I know. Hush, hush,' Sheri murmured. 'We know he's kin, sister. Paneb wouldn't lie about that.'

'Well, more's the pity,' muttered Kia.

Isis and Mut raised eyebrows at each other. Even Ramose was beginning to prick up his ears. Only Kha remained oblivious, solemnly handing Isis pieces of straw to weave into his straw man.

The two women fell silent. Isis finished the straw man and handed it to Kha, who clasped it in delight, then promptly began to pick at the straw, tearing it apart. She eased him off her lap and stood up. Mut looked at her questioningly, but she skipped away without saying anything. Her heart beating a little faster, she went inside, then moved forward along the shadows of the corridor until she could just peek inside the front room.

Sinuhe was in there, as usual. Isis studied him. The peasant was looking at something in his hand, examining it closely. Isis craned her neck, but she couldn't see what it was. She took another step. The peasant was turning the object over in his hands, murmuring to himself. Then he clutched it and brought his hand up to his chest. His eyes were closed. Isis shifted, and her foot brushed a wisp of dry straw on the floor. Sinuhe's eyes flew open.

'Who's there?'

Isis took a deep breath, ignoring the pungent smell that seemed to get richer each day, and stepped inside the room.

'It's Isis,' she said, sitting down beside him. She paused. 'What were you looking at, in your hand?'

Sinuhe's fist tightened against his chest. 'You were spying!'

'No, no, not really,' said Isis. 'I just . . .' She trailed off as the peasant leaned forward, bringing his face close to hers. Isis could see the black pores in his skin, and smell the onions and lentils on his breath. He was frightening, but somehow fascinating, too. She recoiled and scrambled to her feet.

'You little brat,' he growled.

'I was only asking,' said Isis, backing off towards the door. 'I didn't see anything.'

Sinuhe shook his clenched fist at her. 'The gods will punish you!'

Isis was shocked. That was a terrible thing to say! The image of Sinuhe eavesdropping at the top of the stairs flashed into her mind. 'So what happens when *you* spy on people?' she cried. 'Don't the gods care about that?'

Sinuhe glared at her. But, for some reason, he had nothing more to say. Isis backed into the corridor, watching his face. She couldn't work out what his expression meant at first. But then, as he swallowed and gulped, his nostrils flaring, she realised that it was fear.

Hopi let himself into the old priest's courtyard. It was deserted, so he flopped down on the mats.

'Is that you, Hopi?' Menna's face appeared in the doorway. 'You've taken the amulets to Weni?'

'Yes,' said Hopi, rubbing his leg, which had become worse on the way back.

'Good, good. You had no problems, then?'

Hopi looked up at his tutor. 'Me? No, no. I hurt my leg last night, that's all. But you were right to sense something at the embalmers. They do have a problem.'

Menna sat down, giving Hopi his full attention. 'Do they indeed? Tell me.'

Hopi explained that the supplier of natron was letting them down. 'Weni says they have barely enough to cover the bodies,' he said. 'Where does natron come from, Menna? Can't they get some locally?'

The priest of Serqet shook his head. 'The main supply comes from the north. There's a great valley of it there.' He looked thoughtful. 'So this means that my brother's body is in danger.'

Hopi thought of the horrible stench of rotting bodies, but he couldn't possibly tell Menna about that.

'All the bodies I saw were covered,' he said.

'Hmm. Even so, this may be what I detected.' Menna lapsed into silence. 'Well, thank you, Hopi. Now you must go.'

'Go?' Hopi's heart sank. He didn't feel like moving anywhere – in fact, he'd been hoping that Menna might offer to treat his leg.

'You have work to do,' Menna said. 'You haven't finished with the life of scarabs.'

'Oh . . .' Hopi almost groaned. The last thing he wanted to do was trek out to the fields again.

'The magical part of their cycle is the most important, Hopi.' Menna's voice was almost sharp. 'That's what you must come to understand.'

Hopi's shoulders sagged, but he nodded. 'I will do as you say.'

Menna rose silently, and fetched Hopi a beaker of fresh beer. 'Drink this before you go.'

Gratefully, Hopi took the beaker and glugged it down. It was cool and refreshing, and made him feel better. Without too much effort, he got to his feet.

'I'll return later,' he told Menna, and stepped out into the street.

A breeze was blowing from the west, lifting the dust and making it swirl and eddy through the air. Hopi turned his face away from it and began to limp slowly towards the edge of town. But he didn't get far. A breathless figure appeared, barefoot, running towards him.

'Apprentice of Menna!' he cried. 'Is that you?'

Hopi recognised him at once. He was the boy who had been sitting making linen bandages at the embalmers' workshops. 'Yes. Why, what is it?'

The boy gulped and clutched his side, trying to get his breath back. 'Something is missing.'

'*Missing?* You mean –'

'One of the amulets. My master Weni has been through them all. He says that there's no heart scarab – or if there was one, it's gone.' The boy shielded his eyes from a blast of dust.

Hopi's mouth went dry. 'It was there. It was among them, I swear!'

The boy shook his head. 'He has examined them twice. I know how careful he is. He sent me to tell you straight away.'

Panicking, Hopi swung his bag off his shoulder and bent down on one knee to examine its contents, scattering them wildly into the dust. There was very little inside – his papyrus basket, his writing materials, some ostraca – that was all. He turned the bag inside out; nothing more was there. They were still only a few metres from Menna's house. Horror gripped Hopi at the thought of his tutor finding out, and he grasped the boy's arm.

'You mustn't tell Menna,' he pleaded. 'Please, don't betray me. I'll find it!'

'But I must –' began the boy, looking doubtful.

'*Please*,' Hopi begged him. 'I'll be in terrible trouble. I can find it, I know I can.'

He saw a hint of sympathy appear on the boy's face. 'Well . . .'

'You could wait, at least,' Hopi insisted. 'Give me a day.'

The boy relented. 'All right. I'll say I couldn't find you. I'll give you until this time tomorrow. But that's all, or I'll be in trouble myself.'

CHAPTER SEVEN

Isis grasped her brother's hands and gazed earnestly into his eyes. '*He* took it, Hopi. Sinuhe. I know he did.'

Hopi shook his head. 'You don't *know* that, Isis.'

'But it's obvious! He was listening to us when you told me about the amulets. He heard everything. And then I saw him looking at something today – something he wouldn't show me, Hopi.' Isis felt exasperated that her brother wouldn't listen.

'What would Sinuhe want with a heart scarab?' asked Hopi.

'All sorts of things! It's magical and it's made of gold and jasper. It's valuable and he's really poor.' It was as clear as the waters of the Nile to Isis.

But Hopi still wasn't convinced. 'I just don't think it's possible,' he said. 'He would have had to steal it

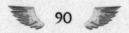

while I slept. That means climbing the stairs, coming on to the roof without waking anyone, going through the box in the dark. Don't you think one of us might have noticed?'

Isis thought about it. It was a good argument, she had to admit. 'So where did it go, then?'

Hopi sighed. 'I think I must have dropped it.'

'*Dropped* it? How?' Isis stared at him.

'At Abana's house,' said Hopi. 'I had my bag with me the whole time, because I didn't want to leave it anywhere. I was careful enough when I climbed into the grounds, but on the way back . . .' He looked over the rooftops, thinking. 'I had to run for the wall. Then I had to climb really fast and scramble over. I fell when I landed, so that must be when it dropped out.'

Isis frowned. This argument made even less sense. 'But how would just one amulet fall out of the box?' she asked. 'Wouldn't they all have tipped out?'

'It was the biggest and heaviest,' said Hopi. 'Maybe that's why.'

'Do you really believe that?' Isis looked at Hopi. Her brother's face was miserable. She knew that this was important, and she hated seeing him upset.

Hopi shrugged. 'It's the only time I didn't take proper care of my bag.'

'So what are you going to do?' Isis felt her heart

quake, because she already had an idea what Hopi would say. And she already knew what she would have to do about it.

'I must go back and look,' said Hopi.

She was right. Isis took a deep breath. 'I'll come with you,' she said. 'I'll distract the guards at the gate, just in case.'

Hopi looked appalled. 'You can't do that. What if Abana sees you? You could end up in a terrible mess. It's all right, Isis – I'll go by myself.'

'No.' Isis could be very stubborn. 'You came with me when I had to go back. It's not your fault that they wouldn't let you in, is it? You tried your best to check on me. Now it's my turn to come back with you. It'll be fine, Hopi. It's not like we have to go inside. You probably won't even have to climb the wall.'

Isis knew that Hopi wouldn't force her to change her mind – they had always backed each other up in the past. Hopi gripped her arm in thanks, and relented.

With the Beautiful Festival of the Valley getting closer, the streets of Waset were full of people bustling around in the afternoon sun. Laughter and chatter filled the air. However, Hopi felt anything but cheerful. He was hot, his leg hurt and he couldn't believe he'd gone and lost something so precious. Now he was going to put Isis in danger, too. He cursed himself inwardly all the way to Abana's long, dusty road with its spacious mansions.

'Now look,' said Hopi, 'if the guards get difficult, I want you to run. Don't stop. Don't worry about me. Just run until you're safe. Is that clear?'

Isis pouted. 'Don't tell me what to do, Hopi.'

'I'm worried about you. I got us into this.'

'I don't think you did. I still think Sinuhe took the scarab. But I know you need to be sure.' Isis touched his arm. 'Come on, let's do it before night falls.'

The wind had dropped and the dust had settled. The sun was beginning to dip; it wouldn't be long before dusk. All was quiet as they walked along the road and stopped at the limestone statue that Hopi had hidden behind before.

'You go on ahead,' said Hopi. 'Start talking to the guards. When you're there, I'll find the place where I climbed the wall.'

Isis nodded. 'Good luck. I hope you find it.'

Hopi watched his sister walk off. Guilt washed over him, then he pushed it to the back of his mind. He had to do the job quickly. As Isis knocked on the gate in the distance, he emerged from behind the statue and followed her, keeping close to the wall. It looked very different in the fading light, but he soon found the spot. He scanned the sandy ground where he had fallen. Nothing. He dropped down on to his knees and swept his hands over the area in case the scarab had buried itself somehow. Still nothing. Feeling panicky, Hopi realised he was going to have to check on the other side of the wall after all.

In a couple of bounds, he had wriggled over the top and scrambled down. He was in. He leaned against the wall, thinking through his actions the night before. In the fig grove, by the grain store and even by the house, he'd been moving very stealthily. He wouldn't have lost the scarab then. But he'd had to dash to the wall and spring upwards; it was most likely that he'd lost it while climbing. He kneeled down and felt around again. Nothing, nothing, nothing. Frantic now, Hopi extended his search. Perhaps it had flown out of his bag and dropped a little further away. He scrabbled around, turning over pebbles and digging into the sand. It was no use. There was no sign of the scarab on this side of the wall, either.

Hopi knew he couldn't put Isis at risk any longer. He hoisted himself back up the wall and managed to drop down on to his good leg. He looked up the road. He couldn't see Isis, but the light was dimmer now.

Perhaps she was hidden in shadow. Slowly, he walked up towards the gate.

It was shut, and Isis was nowhere to be seen.

When Isis heard the gate clank shut behind her, she kicked herself. She should never have let this happen. It had been going perfectly at first: she'd knocked, a guard had answered and, to her relief, it was a man she didn't recognise – he was older, with a kindly face.

'Hello,' she said, 'I'm going to see my uncle, but I think I'm lost.'

The guard smiled. 'Oh dear, that won't do,' he said. 'Do you know which way he lives?'

'Not far from the temples of Ipet-Isut. He's a scribe there, you see.'

'Is he now?' The guard looked impressed. 'Well, you're not too far off track. I can soon point you in the right direction. I'll walk you up the road myself, if you can just hang on a few minutes.'

'Thank you,' said Isis. Waiting a few moments was fine by her – it would give Hopi all the time he needed. She smiled prettily. 'So, who lives in this house?'

The guard laughed. 'Most people know the answer to that question,' he said. 'But maybe you're too young to care about tax collectors.'

'You might be right,' said Isis, laughing with him.

'The work's all right, though,' the guard carried on. 'I'm the day guard, so I go off duty at sunset. Any minute now, you see.' He pointed up at the darkening sky, then beckoned her. 'Just come inside for a minute. I have to go to the house to report that I'm leaving.'

His broad smile had reassured her and, without thinking, Isis had stepped through the gate. Then – *bang*. It had shut.

'You sit here. Won't be long,' the guard called over his shoulder. 'Here comes the night guard. He'll look after you until I get back.'

'I really need to go straight away –' she began.

But it was too late. Isis felt her heart sink. The guard walking towards them was the one who'd been on duty the night before.

'Well, if it isn't our little dancer!' He grinned. 'Couldn't keep away from us, hey?' Then, to her horror, he called after his colleague, 'Tell the boss his favourite dancer is here!'

'No!' Isis turned and pulled at the gate.

The guard put his weight against it, keeping it fast. He had stopped smiling. 'I reckon Abana will be interested to find out what you're doing here.'

Isis gave a trembling smile, and looked appealingly into the guard's eyes. 'Please,' she whispered, 'I was only passing by. Please don't get me into trouble.'

But the guard was unmoved. '*I* haven't done anything,' he said. 'Just my job, that's all.' He looked towards the house. 'Well, well. What about that? Here comes the boss now.'

Isis felt sick. Abana was walking towards her. She made for the gate again, but it was hopeless: the guard would not let her pass.

'Isis. How nice to see you,' said Abana. There was a veiled threat in his voice. 'I think you should come inside.'

'No,' she said. 'I'm not going to. Let me out.'

'But it seems that you came to see me of your own accord,' said Abana smoothly. 'Now you're in a hurry to leave. That's very strange. I think we were talking of favours . . .'

'I don't want anything to do with you,' she spat. 'I know what you are. You're a cheat and a thief.'

Abana's face lost its oily smile. 'Be careful what you say, little she-cat.'

'What I say is the truth! You've got a store full of stolen grain,' raged Isis. 'You take everything from peasants who have lost their crops. You've no right to be the king's servant.'

'She must be silenced. Seize her.' Abana's voice was cold.

The guard made a lunge for Isis, but he hadn't

reckoned on her quick reactions. She ducked under his outstretched arm and ran. In the gathering dusk, she saw the grove of fig trees up ahead and sprinted for it. Her legs flying, she zig-zagged around castor bushes and tamarisk trees, feeling insects batting her cheeks. She reached the grove and dived in among the trees, off the pathway. Glancing back, she saw that she had seconds to spare.

Little she-cat . . . she'd show him.

She leaped at a fig tree, grabbed its lower branches and swung herself up. Scraping her elbows and knees, she pushed herself higher. On a thick branch close to the trunk she stopped. She should be well hidden here. Gasping for breath, she tried to sit still among the broad, green leaves.

The guards crashed through the grove, calling and swearing. Isis thanked the gods that darkness was falling, so they could no longer see her faint footprints in the sandy soil. She leaned against the trunk and waited for silence.

'She's here somewhere! Find her!' yelled Abana's voice, somewhere close by.

But when the guards replied, they were well beyond the grove.

'She must have got over the wall!' one of them called back.

'Damn her,' Abana spoke under his breath. He was right next to her tree.

'No sign of her, master.' One of the guards was returning.

Abana began to move towards the house. 'Leave it. Call off the search.' His voice became a growl. 'I'll deal with this some other way.'

It was almost dark. Bats swooped and dived overhead. Isis knew that for now, all she could do was wait.

The minutes passed, and the darkness became thick and velvety. Then she heard something – a slight scraping – from the direction of the boundary wall. She listened.

'*Isis!*' Her brother's voice was calling, very softly.

Swiftly, nimbly, Isis climbed down the tree and ran towards the sound.

'*Isis!*' came Hopi's voice again.

She could just see the wall, with Hopi's head peering over it. She waved frantically and leaped at it, scaling it in seconds. Then they were both down on the other side, hugging each other.

'I thought he'd got you!' exclaimed Hopi.

'He almost did,' said Isis. 'I hid up a tree. Come on, let's go.'

They ran up the street, Hopi half-hopping as he went.

'Did you find the scarab?' asked Isis, when they finally slowed to a walk again.

Hopi shook his head.

'I knew you wouldn't,' said Isis. 'But don't worry, Hopi. Now I know what I'm going to do. I'll get it back from Sinuhe, I promise.'

The rich smell of roasting mutton floated through the house as they entered. Hopi guessed it was Sheri's idea; she was always the one who tried to cheer the household up, and there was nothing like good food to do that. They went through to the courtyard and found everyone apart from Paneb and Sinuhe gathered around the fire.

'We've got mutton ribs!' shouted Ramose, as Isis and Hopi joined them. 'Sheri and Kia went to the market!'

Hopi sank down gratefully and took the hot, charred rib that Kia offered him. He sat gnawing it, feeling a little strength return. It had been a long day, and he had hardly eaten; the discovery that he had lost the scarab had taken away his appetite.

'Who will take these up to Paneb?' asked Sheri, removing some ribs from the fire.

There was a brief silence. Paneb would normally be eating with them, but since his row with Nefert, he was keeping himself apart. Hopi could still feel the tension in the air. He looked around at the awkward faces.

'I will,' he offered, throwing his bone back into the fire.

He stood, took the ribs from Sheri and carried them up the stairs. Paneb was sitting on his own on the roof, gazing out towards the Nile.

'I've brought you some food.' Hopi handed him the ribs.

'Thank you, but I'm not hungry.' Paneb sighed, and waved them away. 'You eat them, my boy.'

'No, no, I'm not very hungry, either.'

Paneb looked up at him. 'Turning down good mutton? That's not like you. Is something wrong?'

Hopi avoided the question. The two mutton ribs dangled from his fingers. 'What should I do with them?'

'Perhaps we should both make an effort. Come, sit.' Paneb patted the mat next to him. 'Let's eat one rib each.'

Hopi lowered himself down next to his guardian. They ate in silence, ripping the thin shreds of meat from the bones. Paneb finished his, and threw the bone over the low roof wall for dogs or jackals to find.

'I hope you're happy living with us, Hopi,' he said.

Hopi looked at him in surprise. 'Of course.'

'And your studies with Menna are going well?'

'Yes,' Hopi said, with a shrug. 'But . . .' The thought of facing Menna in the morning made him quail inside.

Paneb seemed to be studying him. 'You don't seem very grateful. Believe me, Hopi, you've been very lucky.'

'I'm truly grateful, Paneb! It's just that . . . I fear I've displeased Menna today. He set me a challenge and I've failed.'

'It can't be as bad as all that,' said Paneb. 'Tell me. Perhaps I can help.'

Hopi hesitated. He still couldn't bring himself to admit the loss of the amulet. Quickly, he thought of something else.

'He sent me out into the fields to observe the life of the scarab,' he said, feeling bad, even though he was telling a truth. 'I watched them making dung balls and pushing them into their burrows. But Menna told me that this is only one half of their cycle. I haven't seen the magical half.'

'You don't know what happens?' Paneb sounded surprised. 'Is that what's bothering you?'

Hopi didn't want to tell an outright lie. 'He said I should go and find out, but I haven't.'

Paneb chuckled. 'All that knowledge of snakes and scorpions, and you don't know the ways of the simple scarab.'

In spite of himself, Hopi was curious. 'So what happens?'

In the darkness, his guardian fingered the amulet he wore around his neck. Hopi knew it was a simple faience scarab with a blue glaze; nothing unusual.

'Out of that ball of dung, new life springs forth,' said Paneb. 'This is the scarab's power. It creates itself out of nothing, out of dung and earth.'

'You've seen this?'

Paneb nodded. 'It's an extraordinary sight, the young scarabs coming out of the ground. I am surprised you haven't seen it, Hopi.'

Hopi thought about this. He had grown up in the town, where snakes and scorpions made their way into people's houses and granaries. And he had spent long hours on the fringes of the desert, hunting for more of the same. He had spent *some* time in the fields, of course, looking for snakes among the crops . . . Then it dawned on him.

'You grew up on farmland, Paneb?'

His guardian went quiet for a long, long time. Then

Hopi felt the man's hand on his arm.

'Yes, Hopi,' he said. 'I can no longer deny it, much as I've tried. I grew up toiling in the fields with my family. With Sinuhe. I was born as nothing but a peasant.'

CHAPTER EIGHT

Isis was struggling to stay awake. She was tired, but if she dozed off, all would be lost – she'd be fast asleep right through to the morning. She *had* to stay awake; she had it all planned. She lay back and watched the stars shifting slowly across the sky. The moon had risen, casting ghostly shadows over the softly breathing bodies around her. Paneb was snoring on one side of the roof. Everyone else was quiet; they seemed to be sleeping, too.

At last, she decided it was late enough. She got up and tiptoed silently down the stairs. First she went out into the courtyard and lit an oil lamp from the embers of the fire. Then she fetched the stick she had put aside earlier. With the oil lamp in one hand and the stick in the other, she crept back inside the house. All was dark in the front room. Isis peeped inside, and saw the peasant's form lying prone on the reed mats. He was breathing heavily, fast asleep. Isis placed her own lamp just outside the room, so that it cast only a faint glow, then stepped stealthily forward.

She looked down at the man's face. Even in sleep, a slight frown creased Sinuhe's forehead, as though he could never quite leave his worries behind. He twitched and murmured something. Isis held her breath. But then he was quiet again, and didn't wake. She scanned the floor alongside him, looking for his little linen bundle. It was lying close to his right arm.

Very, very slowly, Isis reached out with her stick and prodded it into the bundle. She fiddled with it, until she was sure that she had caught hold of the fabric. Then she began to pull, easing the bundle towards her.

Sinuhe shifted in his sleep. Instantly, Isis pulled the stick back and stepped out of the room. The peasant turned and slept on. She set to work on the linen bundle once again, this time dragging it further, further, until she could reach down and pick it up. Grabbing the oil lamp, she ran out to the courtyard.

Her fingers trembling with nerves, Isis undid the knot that held the bundle together. The linen was grimy and had the same rancid odour as the peasant himself. Isis wrinkled her nose as the linen came undone. Holding the oil lamp up, she examined what was inside.

The peasant's possessions were few. As far as Isis was concerned, they were nothing but rubbish – bits of broken faience, some twisted scraps of copper, a strip of coiled-up leather. She rummaged for the precious heart scarab. What had Hopi said? Green jasper, cased in gold? Her fingers touched something smooth and rounded. Here it was! Excited, she lifted it out.

However, what she held in the light of the lamp was not made of jasper. It wasn't green and it certainly wasn't cased in gold. It was a scarab, sure enough – or half of one; but it was black, and seemed almost like glass. Frowning, Isis groped around in the linen bundle again. Her fingers found something else. She brought it out and gazed down at another half-scarab just like the first.

She took one half in each hand and put the rough edges together. They were a perfect fit. What she held had once been a beautiful scarab but, somehow, the dark glass had broken cleanly in two.

'You did *what*?'

Hopi felt a rush of affection for his sister. He loved her loyalty and guts, even if they did get her into trouble sometimes. Her nocturnal adventure had left her looking tired, with big hollows under her eyes.

Isis grinned. 'I told you I would.' Then she became serious again. 'I'm sorry, Hopi. You were right. I found a scarab, but it wasn't the one you've lost. It was made of black stuff.'

Hopi frowned. 'A black stone?'

'More like glass.'

'Obsidian.' Hopi thought of the little obsidian blades that Menna used to prepare some of his remedies. 'How big was it?'

Isis made a circle with her finger and thumb. 'Like that. No, a bit bigger.'

Hopi was surprised. 'Are you sure?'

'Yes, of course I am! Why?'

'An obsidian scarab that size is pretty unusual. Obsidian isn't found here in Egypt, it's brought in from other countries. Menna told me so.'

'Well, it's even more unusual now,' said Isis. 'It was broken in two.'

Hopi was intrigued. A broken obsidian scarab . . . could it be part of the mystery that surrounded Paneb and Sinuhe? He was still trying to digest the news that Paneb had given him the night before. He couldn't imagine his guardian working in the fields, or how he had ended up somewhere so different. If you were born a peasant, a peasant you would remain – usually. But, somehow, Paneb had managed to get out of it.

'So it wasn't at Abana's, and Sinuhe didn't steal it,' said Isis, interrupting his thoughts. 'Now what do you think happened to it?'

Hopi sighed. Isis had reminded him that he was no closer to finding the scarab he had lost. He thought of the other information that Paneb had given him.

'Have you ever seen a scarab create itself out of nothing?' he asked his sister.

Isis stared at him as though he'd suddenly gone mad. 'No. Have you?'

'No, but I wish I had.' Hopi stretched in the morning sun. 'The real scarabs do. That's why they're magic. But I don't think the same can happen to amulets. Time's running out, Isis. I'll have to confess to Menna. I can't think what else to do.'

From the rooftop, Isis watched her brother walk along the street. She felt very sorry for him – she knew he was terrified that Menna would be angry. He disappeared around the corner, and Isis sat for a while, basking in the sun. She was tired, but she knew that a lot of preparation lay ahead for the festival the next day. Nefert would appear at any moment, calling her to practise, and Mut would have to try her ankle out, too.

She closed her eyes and dozed off. Then she woke with a start. She really should be helping out downstairs. She got to her feet and glanced at the street again, where someone caught her eye. It was Yuya, their neighbour, walking along with a flagon of beer on her head.

'Yuya!' called Isis.

Yuya put a hand up to the flagon to steady it, and peered upwards. Her face broke into a smile when she saw Isis.

'Isis! How's your visitor?' she called back. 'Did he enjoy the bread?'

'Shhhhh.' Isis gesticulated down to the ground floor. 'He'll hear you!'

Yuya laughed her bubbly laugh. 'Does it matter?'

Isis grinned at her. Yuya was always fun. She was about to shout back when she spotted someone else walking along the street. Someone familiar. It was Abana's night watchman.

'What is it?' Yuya was still looking up at her, puzzled.

The guard was walking slowly up the street, inspecting the crowded town houses as he went. He stopped a woman and seemed to ask her a question. The woman shrugged and shook her head.

The guard carried on. He was getting close now.

'Yuya,' called Isis desperately. 'That man –' She jabbed her finger up the street. 'Tell him I'm not here. Tell him I live that way.' She pointed over the rooftops towards the river. Yuya looked baffled, but Isis could do no more.

She ducked down out of view behind the roof wall, thinking furiously. What could Abana want now? He surely didn't expect Isis to dance for him again? No . . . of course. Isis went cold. She could hear the tax collector's voice: *she must be silenced*. A man like him meant what he said.

Pressing herself against the wall, she tried to hear what was going on down in the street below. There was nothing at first. Then she heard Yuya's voice, loud and clear.

'Dancers? Oh no, not around here. You've come to the wrong part of town.'

The guard's voice was low, and Isis couldn't hear his reply.

'Of course I'm sure!' Yuya's laugh pealed out, giggly and flirtatious. 'I've lived on this street all my life. I know everyone.'

The man's voice murmured again.

'I'd *love* to show you, but I have to deliver this flagon of beer.' Yuya sounded genuinely sorrowful, and Isis sent silent thanks to her friend. 'I'll get into big trouble if I don't. If you go straight to the river and along to the quarter by the temple, I'm sure someone will help you. You ask around there.'

It was perfect. At least two other dance and music troupes lived that way. The guard would have to find them all before he came back here. Silence fell, but she waited a little longer.

'Isis!' hissed Yuya's voice.

Isis peeped over the wall. 'Has he gone?'

'Yes. Who *is* he?' Yuya's face was avid with curiosity.

'Wait there.' Isis ran across the roof and down the stairs. She scanned the street carefully before stepping outside. 'Thank you a million times, Yuya!' she exclaimed, hugging her.

'It was nothing,' said her friend, laughing. 'But whatever's going on? You look scared, Isis,' she added more seriously.

'I *am* scared,' said Isis. 'And I have to go and find Hopi, before it's too late.' She looked at Yuya beseechingly. 'Please don't tell anyone we live here, if they ask. I think I may have put the whole family in danger.'

Hopi walked to Menna's house deep in thought. He wasn't looking forward to telling his tutor about the scarab, but the sooner he got it over with, the better.

Maybe he should offer to repay him in some way – but how, for something so precious? Its magic was surely irreplaceable.

He found the old man in front of his shrine, sitting on his knees with his head bowed. Hopi stood in the doorway quietly, not wishing to disturb him. After a few moments Menna rose.

'Good morning, Hopi,' he said.

'Good morning, master,' said Hopi.

He followed Menna outside and took a deep breath. The moment had come.

'I have things to tell you, Menna,' he said.

The old man raised an eyebrow. 'Indeed? Let's take our usual seat in the courtyard. You can tell me there.'

Hopi's mouth was drying up. As they settled down on to the mats, he found that he couldn't bring himself to confess straight away. 'I've dis-discovered the second half of the cycle,' he stuttered. 'The cycle of the scarabs.'

'Good, good,' said Menna. 'You've seen it?'

'Not exactly,' admitted Hopi. 'But I've found out what happens, and I've reflected on its meaning.'

'To reflect is the most important thing,' said Menna. 'Tell me what you have learned, Hopi.'

'Well, the scarab is a symbol of life,' said Hopi, 'because it creates life from nothing but the ground. I think, I think . . .' He struggled to order his thoughts. 'I think perhaps there are things that we can't fight against. Life will renew itself, regardless of what we might do.' He dried up. Menna was drawing in the earth of the courtyard with his stick.

'Go on,' said the old man.

'That's all,' said Hopi. 'But I wish it were true of stone scarabs as well as real ones.'

'Now you're speaking in riddles,' said Menna.

'I have something to confess.' Hopi bowed his head. 'Forgive me, Menna, for I've lost the heart scarab that you entrusted to me. Weni's messenger came to tell me that it wasn't in the box.'

There. He had said it. He waited for the old man's wrath to explode. But to his surprise, Menna placed a hand on his arm.

'Wait,' he said.

Menna got to his feet and disappeared inside the house while Hopi waited anxiously. When he returned, Menna had a little smile on his face.

'Open your hand,' he instructed.

Hopi held it out, palm upwards.

'Is this what's on your mind?' asked Menna, placing something cool and rounded on to it.

Hopi looked at the object and gasped. It was the green jasper heart scarab, its gold casing glinting in the sun. 'How? Yes!' He looked up at his master. 'You had it all the time?' Now he didn't know whether to laugh or cry in relief. Was it all a mistake, or a trick? 'This has troubled me deeply, Menna!'

'And that is only right,' said the old priest soothingly. 'Don't be angry, Hopi. Let me explain.'

Hopi stared down at the scarab, turning it over and over in his hands. 'But we have risked so much to find it,' he muttered. 'Isis has risked most of all.'

Menna looked at him kindly. 'I'm sorry to hear that, Hopi. I didn't foresee that you would be given the blame. I knew that you wouldn't open the box, and that you'd deliver it safely. This was a test for Weni, not for you.'

A test? So it *was* a trick! Hopi struggled to conceal his feelings. He was furious, however wise Menna might be.

'Before you came to me with news of the natron, I was trying to uncover the problem I had sensed at the embalmers' workshops,' Menna carried on. 'I wondered if Weni was at fault. I wanted to be sure that he was still carrying out his duties. If he noted all the amulets properly, he would know at once that one was missing. But would he care? Once the body was wrapped, I would never know that my brother lacked his most important amulet.'

Hopi listened. *But what about us?* he wanted to shout. *What about Isis?*

'So this has shown me that Weni is honest,' Menna finished. 'It's the problem of the natron that must be resolved –'

He stopped. His words had been interrupted by someone outside.

'Hopi! Let me in!'

Hopi recognised his sister's voice instantly. 'It's Isis,' he said, as once again she hammered on the courtyard door.

Isis continued to bang on the door. This time, she heard Menna's voice.

'Enter!'

She burst through the door and saw Hopi sitting with his tutor on the mats.

'Abana's guard has come looking for me!' she managed to say, gasping for breath.

Hopi stared at her. 'To dance again, you mean?'

'No!' She gulped for air, then ran and flung herself down next to her brother. 'I think it's because of what I told him.'

'What you *told* him? Who, the guard?'

'No, no, Abana,' cried Isis. 'I told him we knew about his grain store and how he steals from all the peasants, and he said I had to be silenced. He said he would deal with me, Hopi. Deal with me *some other way*.' She began to sob.

'Hush, Isis. Calm down.' Hopi put an arm around her. 'Don't panic.'

Isis hiccuped and dried her eyes. 'But we have to *do* something.'

'What's all this, Hopi?' asked Menna. 'Is she speaking of Abana the tax collector?'

Hopi nodded. 'Yes. You've heard of him?'

'Of course.' Menna looked grave. 'What is this about his grain store?'

'Hopi found it when I went to perform,' said Isis. 'Then last night we had to go back. Abana nearly caught me and I told him everything we know . . .'

Menna looked to Hopi for explanation. 'And what *do* you know?'

'The grain store in his grounds is vast,' said Hopi. 'I mean, really vast. Much too big to house his personal supply. We think it holds grain that he has stolen.'

'Such is the way of tax collectors,' said Menna. 'But I had heard that Abana is worse than most. Now I know it's true. What else have you discovered?'

'The rest isn't clear,' said Hopi. 'I saw a man near Abana's grain store, and I heard him say something about shipments. Then I saw him again at the embalmers' workshops. Weni told me who he is. Menna, he's the supplier of natron. He's the one who's letting them down!'

CHAPTER NINE

Menna began to pace slowly up and down the courtyard.

'Very interesting,' he said. 'Well, it's clear enough what's happening. This man you've seen is a trader. He takes Abana's grain north and brings the natron south. That way, he profits from both.'

Hopi thought it over carefully. It was all beginning to make sense. 'So he sells the grain, then collects natron for the embalmers,' he said. 'So why are the embalmers going short?'

'Trading grain – especially stolen grain – must take time,' replied Menna. 'To cover his tracks, Abana probably sells it in small batches. It could take several days to get rid of a whole cargo.'

Hopi frowned. 'But if it takes so long, why doesn't the trader hurry up? He told Weni that he wasn't

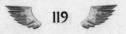

leaving until tomorrow.'

'Tomorrow? But that's the day of the festival!' cried Isis. 'Everyone will be celebrating!'

'Of course!' exclaimed Hopi. 'Moving a cargo of grain down to the river is a big job. But tomorrow everyone will be on the other side, on the west bank. No one will notice the grain being loaded.'

Silence fell for a moment.

'But, Hopi, what are we going to *do*?' demanded Isis. 'Abana's guard is looking for us right now. It won't take him long to come back. What do you think he wants? What will he do to us?'

Hopi didn't know what to say. Abana was powerful enough to do anything, but would he really chase after a dance troupe because they knew about his stolen grain?

'Abana's powerful, but he's not stupid,' said Menna quietly. 'He won't want to draw too much attention to himself. Today the king will be arriving from his palace in the north.'

'So what did the guard come for?' asked Hopi.

'I imagine the plan is to buy your silence. That, at least, will be his first resort,' said Menna. 'He will no doubt combine it with threats.'

'But we'd never let him bribe us!' exclaimed Hopi.

'Paneb might do it for Sinuhe,' said Isis.

Hopi was horrified. 'He couldn't! That would mean protecting the man who's stolen Sinuhe's grain!' he said.

'Yes, but Sinuhe wants repayment,' said Isis. 'This could be Paneb's way of getting it for him.'

'We need time,' said Menna, breaking through their discussion. 'We must consider the best way to deal with this. Isis, you should go and give your family warning. Persuade them to resist Abana, if they can.' He turned to Hopi. 'Meanwhile, you and I have thinking to do.'

Isis ran back through the busy streets, where anticipation about the festival was growing. Women were busy trading the garlands that everyone would wear; boys were dragging great bundles of palm fronds to hand out for people to wave; girls were carrying baskets of lotus flowers and sweet-smelling herbs. The excitement was infectious, in spite of all that was happening.

We're going to see the king, Isis thought as she ran. *We're going to see the king . . .*

She arrived back at her own street and scanned it carefully for Abana's guard. There was no sign of him as yet, so Isis dived into the house.

'Nefert! Paneb!' she called, heading straight for the courtyard.

There was no one there but the two young boys, playing with their toys as usual. Music floated down the stairs; practice had begun. Isis ran to the practice room on the first floor and found the three women in the middle of a melody, while Mut sat on the floor carefully unwrapping the bandage around her ankle.

'Mut! Have you tried walking yet?' For a second, Isis forgot what she had come for.

Mut grinned. 'Yes, I can put my weight on it, I think,' she said. 'But I haven't tried dancing yet. I want to get this thing off first.'

Isis crouched down at once to help her dance partner take off the bandage. Then she helped Mut to her feet as the three women came to the end of their piece.

Nefert looked stern. 'Wherever have you been, Isis?' she demanded crossly. 'You know it's the festival tomorrow. We're very behind as it is.'

Suddenly, Isis realised that if anyone would stand up to Abana, Nefert would.

'Nefert, please don't be angry,' she pleaded. 'I had to go and find Hopi. One of Abana's guards came looking for me – I saw him on the street.'

At the mention of the tax collector, Nefert's lips tightened. 'What did he want?'

Isis bit her lip. 'Well, I can't be sure. I got Yuya to

send him in the wrong direction.' She took a deep breath. 'But Hopi found Abana's stolen grain and . . . and I told Abana that we knew about it.'

'Stolen grain? *You* told Abana – but how . . .'

'Hopi found a big storehouse in the grounds of his mansion. And then we had to go back to look for something,' Isis explained desperately. 'Abana nearly caught me, and I blurted out what I knew. Please, Nefert, we have to do something – Menna thinks he'll try to buy our silence with a bribe but that he might threaten us, too.'

Nefert took a deep breath. 'I've seen how this man behaves,' she said. 'He won't try to *buy* anything. He's too greedy and cruel for that. Well, Isis, it seems that you and Hopi have brought everything nicely to a head. Who knows, it may even be for the best. We must act quickly. Tell both Paneb and Sinuhe that I want to speak with them at once.'

'The first thing to find out is where the loading will take place,' said Menna. 'That's too active a task for me, I'm afraid. It's up to you, Hopi.'

Hopi nodded. 'I'll start at the embalmers' workshops. They may be able to point me in the right direction.' He was still holding the heart scarab. He reached for his linen bag and knotted the precious amulet into one corner. 'I'll take this to them at the same time.'

'Very well,' said Menna. 'But be careful. If you must ask for help, choose who you speak to wisely.'

'I will.' Hopi shouldered his bag and set off.

His leg felt a little better today, and he made his way quickly through the people milling in the streets. At the workshops, he found Weni watching his assistant at work in the second tent, pulling the brain through the nostrils of a new arrival. The stench was worse than ever. It made Hopi feel sick.

'Weni,' he called from the entrance.

The embalmer looked up. 'Good day to you, Hopi. You got my message, then,' he said, coming over.

'Yes, I've brought the missing scarab,' said Hopi.

'Good. Follow me.' Weni led the way to the third tent, where Hopi handed over the amulet. Weni summoned Hetep, and they went through the same ritual as before.

'I wonder if you can help me,' said Hopi, once the transaction was done. 'It may be of great help to you, too. I need to find the boat belonging to your supplier of natron.'

'Really?' Weni looked surprised. 'What is it to you, young apprentice?'

'We suspect him of more than delaying your natron,' said Hopi. 'If we track him down, we may uncover a great injustice. But first, I must find his boat.'

'Very interesting,' said Weni. 'It would be a great relief to have this problem solved. Come.' He led Hopi outside and pointed to the jetty. 'The boat moors there when it brings us the natron. When it leaves, it goes downriver, towards the north. Perhaps that's where you'll find it.'

'Thank you,' said Hopi. 'I hope I'll soon have good news.'

He followed the little path that led down to the wooden jetty, which jutted out well into the river so that a heavy boat could moor. But there was no sign of the boat now. Hopi set off downstream along the shore, thinking. Abana's house must be further towards the temples of Ipet-Isut – and, of course, away from the river towards the desert. The most direct route from the tax collector's grain store to the river would surely end close to here.

The riverbank undulated, and Hopi had to wade through a marshy area where reeds and lotus flowers grew in the shallow water. It was difficult to see ahead through the reeds and Hopi made slow progress, parting them carefully as he went. When he emerged on the other side, he immediately knew he had found what he was looking for. There, up ahead, was a flat cargo boat, pulled in to the side of the river.

The boat seemed to be deserted. Its sails were furled on the two big masts, and there was no one on deck. Hopi stepped back among the reeds again, then followed the marshy area inland up a disused irrigation channel. On the bank, a clump of date palms grew, offering shelter both from the sun and prying eyes. But Hopi could see just enough. Standing in the shade were five donkeys tethered together. And piled in a heap next to them were panniers, perfect for carrying sacks of grain.

Hopi wondered what to do. This could be any cargo boat, any group of donkeys, but that was very unlikely. This was a secret, sheltered mooring and it was in the right place. Eventually, he made his decision, and clambered out of the irrigation channel to take a closer look.

'Hey!'

Hopi was expecting the shout, and stopped. A man had been lying under the palm trees, and now he got up. He brushed himself down and walked over. To Hopi's relief, it wasn't the trader himself, but a rough-looking peasant with rotting teeth.

'What are you doing here?' demanded the man.

'I thought it would be a good place for lotus,' said Hopi. 'It's all been picked further down the river, because of the festival.'

The man grinned. 'That's girls' work.'

Hopi pointed to the scars on his leg. 'Girls' work is all I can do,' he said in a humble voice. Keeping his eyes lowered, he nodded towards the donkeys. 'I expect they'll be going to the festival, too, won't they, sir?'

'What, my donkeys? Nah.' The man shook his head. 'I've been given a big job for them here. Pays better than I've been paid all year.'

'Really? Your employer must be rich.'

'Must be, I suppose. No one in their right mind pays extra to have grain shifted on the day of the festival. Suits me, though.' The man laughed, exposing his blackened teeth.

'I wish you luck,' said Hopi, turning back towards the river.

'And you, you little lotus-picker!'

Hopi smiled to himself as he tramped back down the irrigation channel. This was Abana's trading point – he was sure.

The three sisters looked very imposing, sitting in a row in the practice room. Isis had never noticed before how strong they could seem; they were all tall and beautiful, with expressive features. Their faces usually showed warmth and laughter, but now they were serious, even stern, and there was no doubt that they meant business.

Isis had been the one to tell Paneb and Sinuhe that Nefert wanted to speak to them. Both men came into the room – Sinuhe wary, Paneb defensive.

Nefert didn't waste any time. 'Paneb, enough is enough,' she said. 'Our cousin's arrival has caused us all grief. And now it may bring us even greater misfortune if we don't face up to what's happening to us.'

Paneb looked around at the women's faces. 'And what is that? What's going on?'

'My sisters and I wanted nothing to do with the tax collector Abana. We went to his house because you insisted on it, and all because of your cousin,' Nefert carried on.

Paneb couldn't deny it. 'Yes, that is true.'

'And now it turns out that Abana is every bit as dishonest and ruthless as we suspected him to be. Isis and Hopi have discovered his store of stolen grain, and he wants to make sure they're silenced. His guard is hunting for our house as I speak.'

Alarm spread over Paneb's features. 'Then we must –'

'Wait.' Nefert held up one hand. 'Before we do anything at all, we must settle our own issues. I'm tired of fighting something I don't understand. Why is it that Sinuhe can make such demands upon us?'

Isis and Mut exchanged glances. Isis felt excited and scared all at once. Silence fell, until at last Paneb spoke.

'Very well, I can't hide the truth any longer,' he said.

Isis waited, holding her breath.

Paneb carried on, 'Sinuhe is not a distant cousin. He and I grew up together on the land he now farms. Our fathers were brothers and they both died young.'

Isis stared from one man to the other. They were so very different – Paneb with his soft, plump body and beautiful linen kilt; Sinuhe with his dark, wizened skin and shabby loincloth. She could barely believe it.

'Our grandfather held our birthright,' Paneb continued. 'It was symbolised by an obsidian scarab that had passed down through the generations. I had no wish to lead the life of a peasant and I left . . . I left everything to Sinuhe.'

The scarab that Isis had found! But now it was broken . . .

'You mean you ran away,' said Sinuhe, his voice bitter. 'You left me with nothing but hardship. You left me with your mother as well as my own, and with all our unmarried sisters.'

Isis saw shame creep over Paneb's features. It clearly pained him deeply to think about his past.

'But, cousin, you were given the birthright,' he said. 'You were given the fields. I had nothing. I *was* nothing for a long, long time: a man with no family trade. Believe me, my body grew leaner than yours is now.'

'A young man on his own can always survive,' retorted Sinuhe. 'You fled your responsibilities. I am the one who has toiled year in, year out to grow crops. I am the one who cared for your family. I am the one who bore the greatest burden, and it is a burden I shouldered alone.'

Paneb looked close to tears. 'I am sorry, my cousin,' he said. 'Everything you say is true. I failed my family. I failed you. I should have stayed to help you farm the land and pay the king his taxes.'

It was a tense moment. Everyone was astounded to hear the truth about Paneb's past. Then, to Isis's surprise, Nefert stepped forward and placed her hand in her husband's.

'These were the faults of his youth,' she said to the peasant. 'Paneb has grown up now. He has us. He protects us – a wife and her widowed sisters – and he chose to take two orphans under his roof.'

'That may be so,' Sinuhe muttered. 'But *my* family's belly is empty.'

Paneb seemed to gain strength from Nefert standing at his side. 'You are right, cousin,' he said. 'And believe me, I have been trying to make amends. Your burden has weighed very heavily upon me. But what Nefert says is true: we now face the anger of Abana, and I must protect us all. We have no time to lose.'

Sinuhe nodded reluctantly. 'Very well. I have seen for myself what Abana can unleash on a family. I will do whatever you say.'

'Thank you, cousin.' Paneb looked around at everyone. 'We must leave the house at once,' he said. 'Isis, run to Meryt-Amun's house to see if they will take us in for the night. We'll take everything we need for the festival, and board up the door.'

As the women began to pack away their instruments, Paneb turned to Sinuhe. 'You, my cousin, can rest in the shade on the street, and tell the guard that we have fled.'

Relief spread around the room as Paneb took charge. Isis ran to the door, then looked back to see that Paneb's face was grave.

'Never let it be said again that I have failed to look after my family,' he finished, and drew himself up tall.

CHAPTER TEN

Hopi made his way straight to Menna's house to report back. Out of breath, he let himself into the courtyard and found the old man poring over some old sheets of papyrus.

'I found it!' he exclaimed. 'Menna, the cargo boat is all lined up. Abana has even hired a donkey owner to transport the grain.'

'And is your family safe?'

'I'm not sure – I haven't been back there yet.' Hopi felt a pang of anxiety.

Menna looked grave. 'I hope that Isis has persuaded them it is serious.' He indicated the space next to him. 'Come, sit. I've been doing some research.'

Hopi sat down cross-legged next to his tutor, and gazed in fascination at the rows of hieroglyphs that stretched across the papyrus on his lap.

 132

'What is this, Menna?'

'It's a record of the Beautiful Festival of the Valley, kept by an old friend of mine.'

'A scribe?'

'Of course.' Menna smoothed his hand over the papyrus. 'I've been thinking. The problem we face is Abana's power. There are few in Waset who have the authority to challenge him. The high priests of Amun at Ipet-Isut, perhaps, but I don't think we could reach them. They will be engaged in preparations for the festival and will not be disturbed on any account.'

'So who else is there?' asked Hopi. 'Surely there's someone?'

'Yes, indeed there is.' Menna smiled. 'You must know who arrives in Waset today.'

Hopi stared. 'You mean the king?'

The old man nodded. 'That's right.'

'But . . .' Hopi couldn't quite grasp it. 'How can we reach the king if we can't even reach the priests of Ipet-Isut?'

Menna bent over the papyrus again, pointing to the rows of intricate hieroglyphs. 'My friend's writings have shown me something. Nothing is guaranteed, but there is a chance. Every year the king pays close attention to the performers at the festival.

Sometimes he bestows special favours upon them. He calls the best to speak with his vizier.'

'But that's perfect!' Hopi exclaimed. His heart gave a bound of hope. 'Our troupe *is* the best. I'm sure it is.'

The old man smiled. 'I imagined as much.'

Hopi realised there was no time to lose. He scrambled to his feet.

'I must go at once to tell everyone. They have it in their power to resolve it all!'

Hopi's news set the house of Meryt-Amun buzzing. The trader himself had returned from Lebanon in time for the festival; his wife and daughters served drinks and titbits, excited to be part of the plot.

Isis and Mut were practising their routines in the courtyard under Nefert's watchful eye. They were having to work without music, because it was too risky for the women to play – music was sure to draw attention from the street, where spies of Abana might still be lurking. Isis and Mut did double somersaults, bringing their routine to an end.

'That's enough!' called Nefert. 'You look beautiful, both of you.'

Isis and Mut stopped dancing with relief, and flopped.

'How does your ankle feel?' asked Isis.

'It was sore at first,' Mut admitted. 'But it's fine now.' She wiggled it around, then yawned. 'I'm tired, though.'

Isis nodded. 'I'm going to sleep early. We have to be at our best tomorrow.'

As she spoke, she felt a flutter of nerves. The plot to attract the king's attention was a daring one. What if he didn't notice them? What if they made a mistake? It was all too scary to think about.

She got up and went to find her brother, who was sitting talking to Meryt-Amun about his trips to Lebanon, but excused himself when Isis caught his eye. Together, they went up on to the roof. Isis wanted to hear the rest of the story, and asked Hopi to describe his trip back to the embalmers and his discovery of the cargo boat. When he had finished, she told him what had happened at home.

'So Sinuhe's obsidian scarab is very important,' she finished. 'But he didn't mention that it's broken.'

'Maybe he's afraid,' said Hopi. 'If it's so important, he won't want to reveal what has happened to it.'

'Yes.' Isis frowned. Sinuhe certainly seemed full of fear. 'But at least he listened to Paneb, and did as he said. When we left the house, he sat outside as though he was just a poor beggar until Abana's guard came back. Sinuhe told him that we'd all run away in the night.'

'And the guard believed it?'

Isis shrugged. 'Who knows? He went to tell Abana.'

Hopi grew serious. 'Then we are not yet safe,' he said. 'And the house, too, is in danger.'

Isis looked out towards the sun, which was dipping down in the west. 'Well, let's hope he decides not to strike until he has dealt with his cargo.'

The troupe woke at dawn to begin their preparations. Meryt-Amun's wife and daughters fussed around; Nefert, Sheri and Kia stayed inside to check that their instruments were in tune; Isis and Mut slotted back into their old ritual of helping each other to get ready.

'I'm so glad you're better, Mut,' said Isis, dabbing some red ochre on to her partner's cheeks. 'I never want to perform alone again in my whole life.'

'I hope you won't have to,' said Mut. She grinned. 'I don't like you getting all the attention!'

Isis laughed. It was good to banter, because the butterflies in her stomach were getting worse. She reached for the bronze mirror to show Mut what she'd done.

'Do I have enough eyeliner on?' asked Mut.

'Plenty,' said Isis. 'Any more and it'll smudge.'

They packed away their box of cosmetics. They were ready. Nefert, Sheri and Kia appeared in their translucent linen gowns, and Paneb in his best pleated kilt.

'Come, we must go,' he said. 'And may the gods be with us.'

It was still early, but people were making their way towards the great temples of Ipet-Isut, where the Beautiful Festival of the Valley would begin. Isis knew that the king and priests would already be making offerings to the great god Amun, his son Khonsu and consort Mut, after whom her dance partner was named.

As they drew nearer, more and more people milled around. Isis looked up at the beautiful temples and felt a thrill of excitement. The buildings were awe-inspiring, with their imposing walls painted in the most brilliant colours.

Paneb led the way purposefully to a point near the main gate, where performers were supposed to gather. The king had brought a retinue of his own performers from the north, of course, but this was a chance for the performers of Waset to shine. Together they waited for the great moment when the gates would open.

The atmosphere began to build. The crowd was immense. Many carried offerings for their deceased relatives on the west bank; many others waved palm fronds. Everyone wore garlands around their necks. At last, there was a blare of trumpets and a roar from the crowd as the massive temple gates creaked open. A glorious sight met Isis's eyes – the barque of Amun, carried high on the shoulders of his priests. The god's shrine was dazzling, covered in beaten gold that glistened in the sun.

Behind the barque of Amun came those of Khonsu and Mut. And then came the terrifying vision of the king himself, wearing his beautiful red and white crown. Isis lowered her eyes, not sure she should look. It was one thing to see the shrine of Amun on his barque, but the king was a living god, the gods' representative on earth.

'Don't look away, Isis!' whispered Mut. 'The king's the one we have to impress.'

'Come,' added Nefert. 'It's time to begin.'

As the procession moved forward, the groups of dancers and musicians took up position and joined in, close behind the long retinue of priests. The family troupe began to perform, but this was not yet their moment: they would follow the king over the river, and on the west bank they would get their chance.

A flotilla of boats awaited to take everyone over. First to depart were the royal barques, then the troupe was allowed to climb on to one of the priests' boats. It was a little overcrowded, and Isis gripped Mut's hand as they clambered on board. The river was not her favourite place at the best of times, but now it was covered with boats of all shapes and sizes, and she was frightened that they might clash and tip her in. But as the priests began to sing and the women played their instruments, she realised there was nothing to fear. This was a blessed day, and she would be safe.

On the west bank, the procession made its way to the king's great mortuary temple that sat beyond the fields beneath the towering limestone cliffs. There, at last, it stopped. It was time for the king to assess the performers who had accompanied him on his way.

Nefert made a sign, and the routine began. Isis danced as she had never danced before. It was as though she were in some other world, where dancers never faltered or made mistakes. She and Mut whirled and somersaulted in perfect timing, sometimes landing so close to the king that Isis caught a glimpse of his dark eyes watching her. Then it was all over and they were bowing, trying to disguise their heaving breath.

Lifting her head once more, Isis saw that the king

was whispering in the ear of a man at his side. She and Mut stepped back towards the crowds, but this man approached, telling them to wait.

'May the gods be with you all,' he addressed them. 'The king is most pleased with your performance. You all excel in your arts.'

Isis felt a thrill of excitement. He had noticed them!

'It is his wish that you receive a favour. Is there anything you would like to ask for?'

It was Nefert who spoke. 'Indeed, sir. We have uncovered a great injustice in the town of Waset, and we wish that our king should know of it.'

The messenger's face grew grave. 'You are sure? This is not the sort of request we are used to hearing.'

Nefert's face remained calm. 'Believe me, sir, this is a matter of great importance to us. It concerns one of the king's highest servants. Please, ask him to send a trusted messenger with my dancer's brother. There is no time to waste: the evidence for what I say is unfolding now, even as I speak.'

The vizier's chariot left a cloud of dust in its wake as it careered along the great avenue that stretched between Ipet-Isut and Waset. Hopi clung on, trying to keep his balance as it swayed and bounced on the palm fronds dropped only that morning. The vizier himself held the reins, his concentration centred on his galloping horse.

'Here, here!' shouted Hopi, as he recognised the spot where a little track could be seen on either side of the avenue.

The vizier pulled the chariot to a sudden halt, and Hopi almost fell out.

'I see nothing.' The vizier's voice was curt.

Hopi gulped and got his breath back. 'See, there is a donkey track here. The donkeys are transporting the grain from over there . . .' He pointed towards the desert in the direction of Abana's mansion. 'And taking it down to the riverbank there.'

The vizier looked sceptical. But then, at that moment, the five donkeys appeared around a bend in the track, heavily laden with grain. Behind them, ambling along, was the donkey owner that Hopi had met the day before.

'This is what I expected to find, sir,' said Hopi in relief.

'I see.' The vizier jumped down from his chariot and held up a hand. 'In the name of the king! Whose grain is this?'

The man stopped. Shock and recognition crossed his face as he spotted Hopi, and his eyes boggled at the vizier's finery – the snorting horse, the chariot, the man's linen gown and gold jewellery.

'Nothing to do with me,' he said, his voice panicky. 'I'm just transporting it.'

'I can see that,' said the vizier coldly. 'But where has it come from?'

The donkey owner's gaze flitted between Hopi and the vizier. 'What'll happen to me if I tell you?' he asked.

'That remains to be seen,' snapped the vizier. 'But if you don't, you'll find yourself in trouble. Obstructing the king's orders is a serious offence.'

Alarm spread over the donkey owner's features. 'Humble apologies, sir. It's Abana's grain,' he mumbled. 'Abana the tax collector. He's paid me to take it down to the river. The cargo boat's waiting there.'

'Then it can wait.' The vizier climbed back into his chariot. 'Turn around at once. Take me to this store of grain.' He turned to Hopi. 'You and your family have served the king well. Your actions will not go unrewarded.'

The troupe was making its way back towards the river. The king was still in his mortuary temple, performing his annual ritual. Much of the crowd had dispersed, as now was the time for the wealthier members of society to make offerings to their ancestors in their own individual tombs. Isis looked back at the foot of the limestone cliffs, where people were meandering up between the tomb-chapels that nestled there. She knew that some people would stay overnight, in the hope that their dead relatives would speak to them in their dreams.

None of the troupe had relatives buried in such a special place. Isis thought with sadness that her own parents had not been buried anywhere; they had been taken by the crocodile god Sobek into the depths of the Nile. She brushed the thought aside, and thought instead of Hopi, taking the vizier to see the evidence of Abana's treachery. She could hardly believe that their plan had succeeded – or, at least, it had so far.

Other people were heading home, too, chatting and laughing about the day's festivities. Isis noticed that there was an old man walking in the opposite direction, coming towards them with his back stooped and his weight placed heavily on his stick. There was something familiar about him. Then she realised who it was.

'Menna!' she cried, running up to him. 'Your idea worked! The king blessed us with his favour!'

The old man stopped. 'Well done, Isis. And what has become of Abana?'

'The king was very angry. He sent his vizier to check what Hopi had found,' Isis told him.

The old man nodded. 'I am glad. Now let's hope that order will be restored to our world.' He tapped his stick on the ground and began to walk forward.

'Where are you going, Menna?' asked Isis. 'You missed the festival.'

'I'm too old for such things,' said Menna, with a smile. 'But all the same, this is a day when the family tomb should be visited. And now that I have seen you and heard the news, I can do so with a lighter step, because the embalmers' troubles should be coming to an end.'

'I hope so.' Isis thought for a moment. 'They'll have to find someone else to bring them their natron, won't they?'

'They will. But when the king deals with a problem, he has a habit of doing so thoroughly. I am at peace,' the old man replied.

Hopi returned home to find Paneb lifting down the boards that had blocked the door to their house.

'Hopi!' his guardian greeted him. 'I trust I'm not acting before time. Are we truly out of danger?'

'We are,' Hopi assured him. 'Abana has been arrested by the vizier himself.'

'The gods be praised!' said Paneb. 'Ma'at does not disappoint us.' He placed the last board on the ground and pushed open the door. 'Now, I must go and fetch the rest of the family.'

Hopi wandered inside while Paneb hurried up the road. He had a lot to think about, and he wanted a few moments of peace before everyone returned. Sitting quietly in the front room, he thought of what the vizier had said when he saw the store of grain: 'We must restore this grain to its rightful owners. The king does not steal from his people, for they are his children and he is their god.'

But Hopi wasn't sure how the vizier was going to go about such a huge task, and he wondered what would become of Sinuhe. He frowned as he mulled over what Isis had told him about the peasant and his broken amulet. His mind drifted to the shiny black scarabs he had seen in the fields . . .

Voices interrupted his thoughts, and the family piled through the door in high spirits.

'Hopi!' Isis skipped in with Mut, and the two of them danced around him happily. 'Paneb told us! We're safe!'

They were followed by the women and boys. Hopi

grinned and let his sister hug him, while Ramose and Kha clung to his legs. Then, gently, he extricated himself. While Nefert led the way into the courtyard to begin cooking a meal, Hopi stepped quietly upstairs, looking for Paneb and Sinuhe. He found the two men together on the roof, conversing quietly on the mats. Sinuhe seemed subdued but humble.

'I see that you take care of this family,' Hopi overheard. 'You've learned to take a burden upon your shoulders.'

'I have, cousin,' Paneb responded. 'And I regret that it was not always so.'

Then they fell silent as Hopi approached and sat down next to them.

'I'm sorry to interrupt,' said Hopi. He looked at Sinuhe. 'But I believe there's something that you have not confessed.'

The peasant looked at him suspiciously. 'What do you mean?'

'I speak of the fate of the obsidian scarab,' said Hopi.

Paneb drew in his breath. 'The birthright scarab? What do you know about that?'

Hopi studied his hands, and spoke carefully. 'Paneb, you told me yourself that when a single scarab pushes its ball of dung into the ground, new life springs forth. It is not one scarab that emerges from the ball, but several.' He raised his eyes to Sinuhe's. 'The obsidian scarab is in your linen bundle. It is time to show Paneb what has become of it.'

For a moment, the peasant seemed dumbstruck. Then, slowly, he picked up the bundle that sat by his side and undid the knot. With trembling fingers, he picked out the two halves and held them out in the palm of his hand.

'It's broken!' gasped Paneb.

Sinuhe bowed his head. 'It's the symbol of my birthright,' he whispered. 'I broke it when all was lost.'

'Don't think like this,' said Hopi gently. 'Think that where there was one scarab, now there are two. Take one half, Paneb. You have made up for the errors of your past.'

Paneb hesitated. Hopi saw that he was searching Sinuhe's face, trying to work out if this was what his cousin wanted. Slowly, the peasant nodded.

'Take it,' he said. 'It is yours.'

As Paneb's hand closed over one half of the scarab, Mut's voice rang up the stairs: 'Father! Hopi! There are donkeys outside!'

Paneb, Hopi and Sinuhe looked at each other.

'Donkeys? Where from?' Hopi called back.

'The vizier! The king!'

They all scrambled to their feet and rushed to the rooftop wall. There, down below, were indeed three donkeys. Hopi smiled. They were fully laden with grain.

CAST OF CHARACTERS

CHRONICLE CHARACTERS

Hopi The thirteen-year-old brother of Isis. Ever since surviving the bite of a crocodile in the attack that killed their parents, Hopi has had a fascination with dangerous creatures, particularly snakes and scorpions. He is training to be a priest of Serqet, which will qualify him to treat bites and stings.

Isis The eleven-year-old sister of Hopi. She is a talented dancer and performs regularly with Nefert and Paneb's troupe. Her dance partner is Mut.

Mut The eleven-year-old daughter of Paneb and Nefert, and dance partner to Isis.

Paneb Husband of Nefert, father of Mut, Ramose and Kha, and the head of the household where Isis and Hopi live. He organises bookings for the dance and music troupe.

Nefert Wife of Paneb, mother of Mut, Ramose and Kha, and sister of Sheri and Kia. She plays the lute and is head of the dance and music troupe.

Sheri One of Nefert's widowed sisters, and a musician in the troupe. She has a particularly loving nature.

Kia The second of Nefert's widowed sisters, also a musician living with the troupe. She is slightly more cold and distant than Sheri, but is hardworking and practical.

Ramose Eldest son of Nefert and Paneb, aged five. Mut's brother.

Kha Younger son of Nefert and Paneb, aged two. Mut's brother.

Menna Hopi's tutor, and a priest of Serqet in the town of Waset. (A priest of Serqet was someone who treated snake bites and scorpion stings.)

OTHER CHARACTERS IN THIS STORY

Sinuhe (You say 'Sin-oo-ay') A peasant farmer who works on a small section of land not far from Waset. He is the cousin of Paneb.

Abana The new chief tax collector for the region surrounding Waset. A ruthless and dishonest man who enjoys entertainment and throwing big parties.

Weni The chief embalmer at the embalmers' workshops in Waset. His official title is 'Overseer of the Mysteries'.

Hetep The lector priest attached to the embalmers' workshops in Waset.

Meryt-Amun A trader who lives in Waset, on the same street as Isis and Hopi.

Yuya One of Meryt-Amun's daughters.

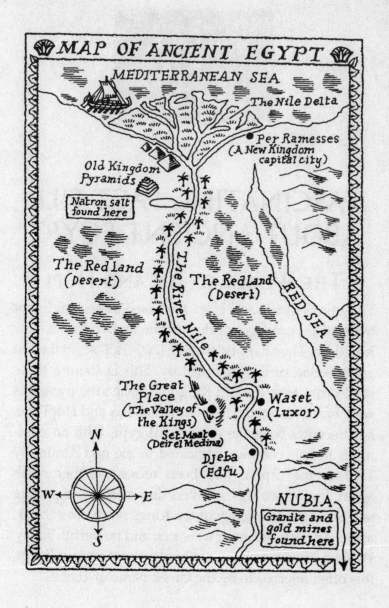

MAP OF ANCIENT EGYPT

MEDITERRANEAN SEA

The Nile Delta

Per Ramesses
(A New Kingdom
capital city)

Old Kingdom
Pyramids

Natron salt
found here

The Red Land
(Desert)

The Red Land
(Desert)

The River Nile

RED SEA

The Great
Place
(The Valley of
the Kings)

Waset
(Luxor)

Set Maat
(Deir el Medina)

Djeba
(Edfu)

N
W — E
S

NUBIA

Granite and
gold mines
found here

FASCINATING FACT FILE ABOUT ANCIENT EGYPT

THE WORLD OF ISIS AND HOPI

The stories of Isis and Hopi are based in ancient Egypt over 3,000 years ago, during a time known as the New Kingdom. They happen around 1200–1150 BC, in the last great period of Egyptian history. This is about a thousand years after the Old Kingdom, when the pyramids were built. Waset, the town in which Isis and Hopi live, had recently been the capital of Egypt, with an enormous temple complex dedicated to the god Amun. By 1200 BC, the capital had been moved further north again, but Waset was still very important. Kings were still buried in the Valley of the Kings on the west bank, and the priests of Amun were rich and powerful. Today, Waset is known as Luxor; in books about ancient Egypt, it is often referred to by the Greek name of Thebes.

A Little Bit about Sacred Scarabs

Scarabs are also known as 'dung beetles' because of what they eat – animal dung. Disgusting? The ancient Egyptians didn't think so. In fact, they thought that some scarabs were so special they were sacred. They were particularly interested in a type of scarab that rolls dung into balls. Lots of scarabs do this, but one kind was common in ancient Egypt. It's now known by its scientific name, *Scarabaeus sacer*, which means 'sacred scarab' in Latin.

The ancient Egyptians believed the sacred scarab was magical because it could create itself out of nothing – well, out of a ball of dung. But they weren't *quite* right. They noticed that the sacred scarab makes dung balls and buries them underground; they noticed that new life (baby scarabs) would appear out of the ground later. But what they didn't realise is that the female scarab lays eggs inside the dung balls, and that this is where the new life comes from.

The ancient Egyptian scarab god, Khepri, was the god of the rising sun. If you look at a picture of a scarab rolling a ball of dung along, it's easy to understand why – a dung ball looks perfectly round, just like the sun. The Egyptians imagined that a giant scarab pushed the sun up over the horizon each morning. A new day was another form of rebirth, making the scarab doubly magical.

Because of the scarab's links with new life and rebirth, Egyptians believed that scarab amulets had strong protective powers. Many people wore them to ward off evil or sickness. Most scarab amulets were quite small; many were made from the glazed ceramic substance called faience. But some scarabs had a special function – for example, heart scarabs. These were usually larger than the amulets worn every day, and were made of stone. Heart scarabs were supposed to have a gold casing, too, like the one in the story, but most people couldn't afford that. They were for placing over the heart of a dead person, and they often had a verse from the *Book of the Dead* written on the flat side underneath. The *Book of the Dead* said that heart scarabs should be made out of a particular stone called *nemehef*, which may be green jasper, although no one is totally sure. In practice, a variety of stones were used, including serpentine and obsidian.

Scarabs, like most beetles, have wings – they can fly. Occasionally, scarabs were shown with their wings outstretched. Winged scarab amulets, like heart scarabs, were usually made to be placed in people's tombs.

MAKING MUMMIES

'Embalming' is just another way of saying 'making a mummy'. Both these terms mean trying to preserve a body so that it doesn't rot when a person dies. Ancient Egyptians mummified dead people because they believed that they would need their bodies in the Next World. They are famous for their embalming techniques, but actually it was an expensive process; most ordinary people couldn't afford to have it done. So the majority of the mummies that have survived to this day are the bodies of important people, like kings, queens and wealthy officials.

The most elaborate embalming method took about seventy days. First, the embalmers washed and shaved the body. Egyptians didn't think the brain was very useful, so they removed it with a hook pushed up through the nose and threw it away. Next, they made a slit in the side of the body and removed most of the organs – the lungs, liver, stomach and intestines. These were dried out separately and placed in four jars (canopic jars). The heart was thought to be the most vital organ of all, so it was always left inside the body.

To dry the body out, the embalmers used special salt called natron, which is found in large quantities in the dried-out lakes far to the north of Waset. The body was covered and stuffed with the salt, then left for about 30–40 days. When the natron was removed, the body was ready at last to be anointed with oils and resins, stuffed with more natron and linen, and wrapped tightly in linen bandages. Bandaging the body was a big job. It could take about two weeks to do it properly, and the embalmers inserted amulets in between the strips of linen to protect the body in the Next World. The heart scarab amulet was the most important one.

Once it was fully wrapped, the body was ready to have a mask fitted over the face. Then it was placed in a coffin for the funeral, which involved many spells and rituals to ensure that the person would make it safely to the Next World. Inside their tombs, the richest people had a stone coffin called a sarcophagus, into which the wooden coffin was placed.

For poorer people, there were cheaper mummification options. One was quite gruesome: the embalmers injected lots of cedar oil into the body, stopped up all the obvious openings, then waited for the oil to dissolve the internal organs. The stoppers were then removed and the sludge was allowed to flow out. After that, the body could be dried out further with natron. The cheapest option of all was to leave the body intact, but to dry it out as much as possible with natron before preparing it for burial.

Farming Life

Farming life in ancient Egypt revolved around the flooding of the River Nile, which happened every year in the season of *akhet* or flood, beginning in June and ending in October. Everyone waited anxiously for the waters to rise – the higher the better, because then more land could be farmed. For peasant farmers, the flood provided a time of rest – unless they were summoned by the king to work on one of his building projects! Slowly, the waters receded, leaving behind a layer of rich black silt, ideal for growing crops. In October, when the fields were dry enough to plough again, the season of *peret* began – the season of 'emergence', when farmers sowed their seeds and watched the first shoots poke their heads through the rich earth. By the month of February, the crops began to ripen and the third and final season began – the season of *shemu*, or harvest.

It was very important for the ancient Egyptians to have a large harvest of grain – bread made from emmer wheat was their staple food, and beer made from barley was their main drink. There was only one grain harvest, so they had to grow enough to last all year. Much of the land was owned by the king, or by wealthy temples and high officials, who all had peasants to work the land for them. It's thought that these peasants were not allowed to move or find other work, even if the land itself changed hands. But there were some independent farmers, too, who had to pay the king a portion of their crops in taxes. In this story, Sinuhe and Paneb's family have farmed a small portion of land for generations, so they feel it is 'theirs', but the king could no doubt claim it if he wanted to, and they still have to pay the heavy taxes.

The farming life was hard. Farmers not only had to deal with mice and rats, but also occasional swarms of locusts, which could devour an entire crop in minutes. It was also true that there were dishonest tax collectors who took more of the crop than they were supposed to.

FAMOUS FESTIVALS

The ancient Egyptians loved parties and celebrations, and there were festivals all year round, too. Most of them were in honour of a god or goddess, or to mark an important event in the calendar, such as the harvest or the new year. Some festivals happened all over the country, whereas others were based in a particular town.

In Waset, there were two major festivals every year: the Festival of Opet, and the Beautiful Festival of the Valley, which is the one described in this book. Both festivals revolved around the great temples of Ipet-Isut (now known as Karnak), home to the great god Amun, his consort Mut and her adopted son Khonsu, the moon god.

The Festival of Opet was a fertility festival that took place during *akhet*, the season of the flood, when there wasn't much farming work to do and everyone could join in the fun. By the later part of the New Kingdom, the festivities lasted for weeks. They began with a grand procession of statues of the gods from the temples of Ipet-Isut down to the River Nile, where *barques* would carry them upstream to another big temple called Ipet-Resyt, in the town of Waset itself (this is now called Luxor Temple). After many secret fertility rituals inside the temple, the gods were carried back to Ipet-Isut again. Of course, they were followed by singers, dancers and musicians, priests and nobles, and throngs of happy people.

The Beautiful Festival of the Valley celebrated the reunion of the living with the dead. Like the Festival of Opet, it started at the temples of Ipet-Isut, and again the gods were carried out on the shoulders of priests. But this time, they were taken over the River Nile to the mortuary temples on the west bank. While the king and priests observed rituals inside the

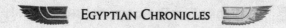

temples themselves, anybody who had a family tomb in the area would visit it to make offerings to their ancestors. Everyone wore garlands of fresh flowers to encourage the dead to communicate with the living. People brought a feast of food and wine to the little tomb-chapels, and stayed up all night celebrating.

GODS AND GODDESSES

Ancient Egyptian religion was very complicated. There wasn't just one god, but hundreds, each symbolising something different. Many of them were linked to a particular animal or plant. The Egyptians believed that their king or pharaoh was one of the gods, too.

Not everyone worshipped the same gods. It would have been very difficult to worship all of them, because there were so many. Some gods were more important than others, and some places had special gods of their own. People would have had their favourites depending on where they lived and what they did.

These are some of the most important gods of the New Kingdom, and all the special ones that are mentioned in this book.

163

Amun The great god of Waset (Thebes), a creator god and god of the air. When Waset became very powerful in the New Kingdom, he was combined with the sun god Re and became **Amun-Re**. He was shown with tall feathers on his head, or with a ram's head.

Anubis The god of mummies and embalming. He was usually shown with a jackal's head.

Apep The great snake god of darkness, chaos and evil. He was usually shown as an enormous serpent, but sometimes as a crocodile or even a dragon.

Bes A god who was worshipped in people's homes, rather than at shrines and temples. He was shown as a bearded dwarf, often with his tongue sticking out, and was believed to protect people's houses, pregnant women and children.

Hapi The god of the Nile, specifically the Nile flood that happened every year. Although he was a male god, he was shown with large breasts because he represented fertility.

Hathor A goddess of fertility, love, music and dancing. She was usually shown as a cow, or a woman with a cow's head, or a woman with a cow's ears and horns.

Horus The falcon-headed king of the gods, who fought and won a battle with his evil uncle Seth. The reigning king of Egypt was believed to be the embodiment of Horus.

Isis The mother of Horus and wife of Osiris, the goddess of motherhood and royal protection. She was associated with the goddess Hathor.

Khepri The scarab god, the god of the rising sun. It was believed that he pushed the sun up every morning in the same way that a scarab pushes its ball of dung.

Khonsu The moon god of Waset, worshipped in the great temple complex there. He was the adopted son of Mut.

Ma'at The goddess of truth and justice, balance and order, who helped to judge people's hearts after their death.

Mut The great mother goddess of Waset, worshipped with Amun and Khonsu. Because Waset is often called Thebes, these three are known as the 'Theban Triad'.

Osiris Husband of Isis, father of Horus and brother of the evil god Seth. He was the king of the underworld, so he was usually shown as a mummy.

Re (or **Ra**) The sun god, who travelled across the sky every day in a *barque* (boat).

Serqet The goddess of scorpions. She was believed to cure the stings and bites of all dangerous creatures like snakes and scorpions.

Seth The brother of Osiris, the god of chaos, evil and the Red Land (the desert). He was shown with the head of a strange dog-like creature that has never been identified.

Sobek The ancient Egyptian crocodile god. On the whole, he was feared by the Egyptians, but he was sometimes seen as a god of fertility, too.

Tawaret A hippopotamus goddess who protected children and women, particularly during childbirth. Like Bes,

Tawaret was worshipped in people's homes rather than in temples.

Thoth The god of writing and scribes. He was shown as an ibis, or with the head of an ibis.

GLOSSARY

acacia A small, thorny tree. Some types of acacia grow particularly well in dry, desert regions.

amulet A lucky charm, worn to protect a person from evil.

ankh The ancient Egyptian symbol of eternal life. It is a cross with a loop at the top. Amulets were made in this shape, and gods were shown holding an *ankh* in tomb paintings.

barque The common term for an ancient Egyptian boat, particularly a religious or royal boat. They were usually slender with an upturned prow, and had lots of uses, from carrying the king to transporting statues of the gods during festivals. In ancient Egyptian religion, Re travelled across the sky in a barque each day, and the dead used the same barque to reach the Next World.

Black Land The rich, fertile land close to the Nile, where the ancient Egyptians felt safe. They lived and grew their crops here.

Book of the Dead Not really a book, but a collection of spells, hymns and instructions for making sure a dead person arrived safely in the Next World. The name 'Book of the Dead' was made up by an Egyptologist. The Egyptians had another name for it that roughly translates as 'Spells of Coming Forth by Day'.

canopic jar Protective jar used to hold the internal organs of mummies. There were always four for every mummy: one each for the liver, stomach, lungs and intestines.

castor A shrubby plant widely grown in ancient Egypt. Its seeds were used to make castor oil, which the Egyptians rubbed on their skin and hair to make them glossy, and burned as a fuel in oil lamps.

clerestory window A window set high in a wall to let in some light. Only big houses had windows – most people's houses were very dark inside to keep them cool.

djed **pillar** A strange-looking symbol, like a little tower with ridges at the top, that meant 'stability'. Amulets were made in this shape.

emmer wheat The type of wheat that was grown in ancient Egypt. Barley was the other main food crop.

faience A sort of ceramic with a coloured glaze (often blue), used to make jewellery and amulets.

hieratic A shorthand version of hieroglyphics, which simplified the hieroglyphs to make them quicker to write.

hieroglyphics The system of ancient Egyptian picture writing. Each individual picture is called a **hieroglyph**.

Ipet-Isut The ancient Egyptian name for the great

temple complex just to the north of Waset, now known as Karnak.

Ipet-Resyt The large temple complex in the town of Waset, connected to Ipet-Isut by a long avenue lined with sphinxes. Like Ipet-Isut, it was dedicated to the worship of Amun, Mut and Khonsu. It is now known as Luxor Temple.

jasper A popular gemstone in ancient Egypt. As well as green, there were red, brown, black and yellow varieties. It is thought that the *nemehef* stone, prescribed in the *Book of the Dead* for making heart scarabs, may be green jasper.

Kingdom of the Dead Generally speaking, the west bank of the Nile was seen as the Kingdom of the Dead because the sun sets to the west.

kohl A kind of dark powder that the Egyptians used as eyeliner to outline their eyes.

lector priest A priest who read or spoke the rituals and spells in a temple or other holy place.

limestone Along with sandstone, this was a rock commonly found in Egypt and used to build the many temples (but not houses, which were made of mud brick).

lotus Lotus flowers were actually blue water lilies that grew along the Nile. Their flowers open in the morning and close at night, so they were seen as a symbol of the rising and setting sun, and the cycle of creation. They were used in perfume, and were believed to have healing powers, too.

ma'at The ancient Egyptian principle of divine justice and order. The principle was represented by a goddess of the same name.

mortuary temple There were two kinds of temple in ancient Egypt. Cult temples were for the worship of a particular god or gods, while mortuary temples were for the worship of a king after his death. Mortuary temples were mostly found on the west bank – the Kingdom of the Dead.

natron A kind of salt mixture that was found on the beds of dried-up lakes in the desert. It was good at soaking up moisture, so it was used for drying out bodies in the embalming process. It was also used as an everyday cleaning agent.

Next World The place ancient Egyptians believed they would go after death. It would be better than this world, of course, but quite similar – which was why they needed to take their bodies and many possessions with them.

Nile flood Also called the 'inundation'. Every year, the Nile river flooded, covering the fields with rich black silt. When the waters went down again, the farmers could plant their seed.

obsidian A kind of dark (often black) glass that forms naturally in volcanoes. It didn't occur in Egypt, so it had to be imported. It could be used to make very sharp blades, as well as ornaments and amulets.

ostracon (pl. **ostraca**) A small piece of pottery or a flake of limestone used as 'scrap paper' for writing on.

papyrus A kind of reed that used to grow in the marshes alongside the Nile, especially in the Delta region to the north. It was made into many things – mats, baskets, sandals and even boats – but it is most famous for the flat sheets of 'paper' made from it, which are named after the reed.

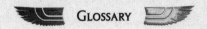

pharaoh The ancient Egyptian term for their king. It was only used by the Egyptians themselves in the later stages of their history, but we now use it to refer to any ancient Egyptian king.

Red Land The desert, the land of the dangerous god Seth. It was greatly feared by the Egyptians because it was impossible to live there.

red ochre A red-coloured clay that the Egyptians ground up to make lipstick and blusher. They probably mixed it with oil or fat to put on their lips.

sarcophagus A big stone coffin. A smaller wooden coffin was often put inside.

scarab A kind of dung beetle that was worshipped by the Egyptians. Scarab amulets were thought to give great protection. The scarab was the creature of the god Khepri (see the Gods and Goddesses section).

tamarisk A small bush or tree that grew in ancient Egypt, with pretty pink or white flowers.

tomb-chapel The little chapels that were built over a person's tomb, where relatives could visit, pray and make offerings.

udjat **eye** The eye of Horus, a symbol of healing and protection. In Egyptian myth, it was the eye that Horus lost in a battle with his evil uncle Seth, but which was healed by the god Thoth.

vizier The ancient Egyptian kings' second in command, who often presided over important trials.

Isis and Hopi's thrilling story continues,
as they help a wounded soldier and
a prisoner of war in

THE DEATHSTALKER

Read on for an exciting extract . . .

EGYPTIAN CHRONICLES

THE DEATH STALKER

It was Isis who heard them first.

'Listen!' she said, grabbing Mut's arm.

The two girls sat still as the noise grew closer. Hoof beats and rhythmic tramping, then the blast of a trumpet.

Isis scrambled to her feet. 'Come on!'

'We can't,' protested Mut. 'We have to wait for Mother's washing . . .'

But Isis was already running away from the river-bank and up the street. 'We'll come back afterwards!' she shouted over her shoulder.

She ran on into the town, where the commotion was getting louder. Mut caught up with her and they joined hands, weaving in and out of the crowds that were beginning to gather.

'Is it the king?' called a woman from a doorway.

'No, no,' a man called back. 'It's the army! They're celebrating a victory!'

'Victory! Victory!'

The cry went up along the streets, and Isis felt her pulse quicken with excitement.

She and Mut made their way to the temple that dominated the centre of Waset. Both of them were dancers, small and supple, so it was easy to duck and wriggle their way through the milling people. Isis caught sight of chariot wheels, then peered around a man's shoulder to see ostrich plumes bobbing on horses' heads.

'Nearly there,' she said to Mut, and they dived forward one last time.

The rich, tangy smells of leather and sweat hit her nostrils as they emerged from the edge of the crowd. A row of five chariots clattered towards them, the horses prancing and tossing their heads, the drivers' arms bulging with muscles as they tugged on the reins. Behind each chariot driver stood a proud soldier, waving a spear or a bow, encouraging the throng to cheer them on.

One chariot rode slightly in front of the others, and Isis noticed that its soldier was the only one wearing armour. 'We are the fighters of Amun!' he cried. 'He has given us victory again! Praise Amun, people of Waset!'

'Glory to Amun!' roared the crowd.

The chariots passed by, and behind them came a platoon of infantry – five rows of ten men marching in perfect time, each with a spear in one hand and a shield in the other. Isis saw that some of them had raw-looking cuts on their arms and chests, but they showed no pain on their faces.

'They're so brave,' she whispered in Mut's ear.

Mut nodded, her eyes wide with admiration.

The company had come to a halt, and up ahead, the leader was making an announcement.

'What's he saying?' Mut demanded, of no one in particular.

The news filtered along the crowd. 'They've set up camp on the outskirts of Waset,' someone told them. 'They found Libyan marauders in the desert and defeated them, so they have come to give thanks at the temples here.'

Mut gripped Isis's hand more tightly. 'Did you hear that? They're camping here. You know what that means!'

Isis was puzzled. 'What?'

'They'll be looking for entertainment,' said Mut. 'We must tell Father. He could ask if they'd like to see the troupe. Wouldn't it be wonderful to perform for them?'

'Oh *yes*.' Isis grinned. It was a brilliant idea. 'Let's go right now and find him!'

Hopi heard the troops from further away – a drifting cacophony from the direction of the river as he and his tutor Menna prepared to go out on a visit.

Menna smiled. 'They like nothing better than the adulation of the crowds,' he commented. 'And why not? They have earned it.'

'Who are they?' asked Hopi.

'I heard that it is a company of the division of Amun,' said Menna. 'Just five platoons.' He grasped his walking stick. 'Come.'

Hopi followed Menna along the winding streets, listening to the distant noises. Menna was old and could not walk fast, but somehow the thought of fit, marching soldiers made Hopi all the more conscious of his own limp. It had been over five years since the jaws of a crocodile had inflicted his wounds, and they had healed as well as they ever would. He was lucky to be alive at all, but when he thought of able-bodied men and boys, he felt a pang of envy all the same.

Menna stopped at the door of one of the larger town houses, and knocked.

'My old friend Anty lives here,' he said. 'He is a wise and well-respected scribe. He has summoned me – to celebrate the return of his son, no doubt.'

Hopi was surprised. He had imagined they were on a mission to treat someone for a snake bite or scorpion sting – that was what they usually did. But now, a servant opened the door and Menna entered. Hopi stepped in after him, noticing at once that this was the house of a wealthy man. It was lofty and spacious; fine murals were painted on the walls, while beautiful carvings and furniture were dotted about the rooms. A middle-aged man appeared from one of them and extended his arms in greeting.

'Menna, may the gods be with you. Life, prosperity, health!' he exclaimed. 'You have not come a moment too soon.'

'Anty.' Menna accepted the man's embrace, then stood back and surveyed his friend's worried expression. 'I had expected a celebration. Is something wrong?'

The scribe wrung his hands. 'I fear so, I fear so. Djeri has returned, sure enough. But he is wounded, Menna. They have brought him here.'

Menna seemed startled. 'He is not with his platoon?'

'No, no. That is why I called for you. Come.'

The two men hurried through the house, still talking.

'But I am not a doctor, Anty,' Menna was protesting.

'I know that, old friend, I know that.' Anty placed a hand on Menna's shoulder. 'The doctors have already been. But you have skills, nonetheless, you have powers, you are a priest . . .'

They entered a cool, dim room at the back of the house. A young man lay there, his eyes closed. Hopi stared. There was a deep gash on the man's shoulder, surrounded by red, swollen flesh. And that was not all. Hopi's eyes travelled down his body to the linen sheet that was draped over his legs. One of them bulged with bandages, but in spite of all the coverings, there was still blood and pus seeping through. Hopi didn't need to see any more to know that these were no minor wounds. This was serious. He was looking at a soldier who was very badly injured.

THE DEATHSTALKER
by Gill Harvey
COMING SOON